# The Universe Had Other Plans!

Versha Dabas Sangwan

**BLUEROSE PUBLISHERS**
India | U.K.

Copyright © Versha Dabas Sangwan 2025

All rights reserved by author. No part of this publication may be reproduced, stored in a retrieval system or transmitted in any form or by any means, electronic, mechanical, photocopying, recording or otherwise, without the prior permission of the author. Although every precaution has been taken to verify the accuracy of the information contained herein, the publisher assumes no responsibility for any errors or omissions. No liability is assumed for damages that may result from the use of information contained within.

BlueRose Publishers takes no responsibility for any damages, losses, or liabilities that may arise from the use or misuse of the information, products, or services provided in this publication.

For permissions requests or inquiries regarding this publication, please contact:

BLUEROSE PUBLISHERS
www.BlueRoseONE.com
info@bluerosepublishers.com
+91 8882 898 898
+4407342408967

ISBN: 978-93-7018-933-1

Cover Design: Vanshita
Typesetting: Pooja Sharma

First Edition: June 2025

*To Nitin, my dear husband—*

*my constant, my wind, my strength.*

*Thank you for never letting me stop dreaming.*

*And to Bella—our dog, my silent companion through every late night*

*and early morning. You never left my side.*

*This book carries your warmth between the pages.*

# Author's Note

This book started as a whisper in my head—and stayed there for years.

Aarohi's character lived in my heart long before I ever put her on a page. I kept telling myself I wasn't ready. That I didn't have the time, the courage, or maybe even the talent to write a book.

And then, I met my husband, Nitin—four years ago.

Loving him, knowing him, and seeing the layers of who he truly is inspired me to write Arjun. The vulnerable side of a man—the kind of strength that doesn't always roar.

In many ways, writing this book helped me heal parts of myself I didn't even know were wounded. I poured in my fears, my dreams and my questions about love, purpose, success, and timing.

And if even a single line in this story makes you feel seen— makes you pause or gives you a little hope—then this book has done what I hoped it would.

Thank you for picking it up.

Thank you for giving Aarohi and Arjun a little space in your world.

And thank you—for reading the words I was once afraid to write.

*With all my heart,*

Versha

**P.S.** If this book finds you at a time when you're hurting—hold on. The universe might just be rearranging everything for you.

*For the ones standing at the edge of what was—*

*You were certain once.*

*About love, about dreams, about where life was meant to go.*

*But certainty is a fleeting thing,*

*and the road you walked so sure-footed*

*has vanished beneath your feet.*

*Maybe you lost what you wanted most.*

*Maybe the universe closed doors*

*before you ever had the chance to walk through them.*

*But here you are.*

*Breathing, moving, becoming.*

*And perhaps, this is not the end of your story—*

*just the chapter where you learn*

*that what's ahead is not a loss, but a beginning.*

*The universe had other plans.*

*And one day, you'll understand why.*

# Chapter 1: I saw him.

## Aarohi

*Romeo, take me somewhere we can be alone.*

*I'll be waiting: all that's left to do is run.*

*You'll be the prince, and I'll be the princess.*

*It's a love story, baby, just sayyyyyyy, "Yesssssssssssssssssssssss!"*

Sssssss... Singing Taylor Swift at the top of my lungs like I'm on the Eras Tour, it hits me—oops, it's 5:40 a.m. Half the world is still sleeping. And here I am, probably scaring my neighbours. Again.

Am I a morning person? Ha. No. But somehow, this daily run has become a ritual.

*(Okay, okay—that's a lie. Every morning, I tell myself: "Just one more day"—just one more, to keep going for my marathon commitment this year.)*

I've made this promise to myself *too many times* on January 1st, only to get distracted. Once, I even came super close—only to end up volunteering at the marathon instead of running it.

*(Yup, that's me.)*

I pull on my black leggings, a loose tank, and zip up my pink running jacket—Delhi mornings are chilly. Phone, check. AirPods, check. Crap—watch battery at 5% again. Ugh!

*Can you even call it a run if it's not tracked?*

No time to dwell—I'll rely on my phone for tracking today.

Jogging through the winding streets, the crisp morning air nips at my cheeks. My route takes me through the cantonment area which crosses past the military hospital, then cuts across a small football field—usually empty at this hour, just a patch of grass in the dim morning light.

*It's an easy-peasy recovery run today*, as per the Nike Run Marathon Series, but nothing about today *feels* easy. My legs are sore from last weekend's 15K long run, and I swear I need someone to stretch me out.

And *then* I see him.

Cue dramatic slow-mo, internal violins, and me pretending not to trip over my own feet.

A figure dressed in all black—T-shirt, shorts, sneakers—sitting by the fence. Next to him, crutches are propped up against the metal bars.

*Who works out on crutches?*

I slow down slightly, pretending not to stare (*but totally staring*). He's lying on his back, doing ab crunches with such fierce concentration. His trim beard frames a sharp jawline, and even from a distance, I can feel his intensity.

There's a calm aggression in the way he moves.

And for some reason, my heart gives the tiniest flutter.

*You're sweating. You're red. Just run, Aarohi. Don't be weird. Don't do finger guns.*

I pick up my pace and hurry forward, but for the rest of my run, I can't get him out of my head.

By the time I reach home, the sun has climbed higher, painting golden streaks across the rooftops. My legs ache, my ponytail is a mess, and I can already feel the soreness creeping in from last week's long run.

Straight to the bathroom. Shower on. Ice cold. The water stings at first, but I let it run, washing off the morning sweat and whatever thoughts are lingering.

By the time I step out, towel wrapped around me, my dressing table is already a war zone—tiny glass bottles of industrial fragrance oils everywhere. Some labeled, some not.

I reach for Vanilla Caramello, spritzing it on my wrists and neck.

**Top notes:** Vanilla, Pistachio

**Middle notes:** Heliotrope, Jasmine Petals

**Base notes:** Salted Caramel, Sandalwood

I pull on my white blouse, tailored trousers, and low heels. Hair up in a loose twist, a quick swipe of lipstick, and I'm out the door.

Delhi traffic was its usual circus—horns blaring, autos squeezing into gaps that shouldn't physically exist. With my older brother off to Canada, his XUV practically became mine.

I gripped the steering wheel and let out a deep breath. *Just get me to work in one piece.*

The drive to Evora Events—an event management SaaS company where I work as a Project Manager—usually takes about forty minutes.

(Assuming Delhi doesn't throw one of its "surprise" jams at me today.)

I tap my pen against my desk, staring at my screen.

Inbox? Full.

Pending approvals? Stacked.

VIP passes? Still untouched.

But—

*Will he be there tomorrow?*

Aarohi. Focus.

I blink, shake my head, forcing my eyes back to the screen—work, priorities, deadlines. But he lingers, like a song stuck in my head. I don't remember the lyrics, I don't even know his name... and yet, I can't get him out of my mind.

# Chapter 2: Utter Chaos

## Aarohi

Somehow, I've started caring way too much about what I wear on my runs.

Suddenly, I'm evaluating all my leggings. The black ones fit best, but do they really make my glutes pop? What about my tank tops? The loose one? No. The snug one? Maybe. And, oh my god, am I actually matching my socks? Who even does that?

And then comes the real madness.

*I cleaned my running shoes.*

*Like actually wiped them down.*

*For the first time since... ever.*

I groan, staring at my reflection in the mirror. "Oh god, what is wrong with me?" I mumble.

No answer. Just the same girl staring back. Same messy ponytail. Same eyes over analyzing every angle.

For what?

For nothing.

For no one.

Except maybe to not look like a complete disaster if I happen to run past... someone.

Ugh. I need to go before I drive myself insane.

..................................................................................

Day two. He's not there.

The football field is just... empty.

Maybe I dreamt him up? The thought is ridiculous!

..................................................................................

Then, on the third... or fourth morning (honestly, I've lost count), I jog around the same curve—expecting nothing.

And that's when I see him.

Oh.

Black-on-black. Crutches leaning against the fence.

The early sunlight hits his face, casting sharp shadows along his jaw. His broad shoulders tense, core tightening with each slow, controlled crunch. The fabric of his black T-shirt stretches against his back, against the solid, unfairly strong frame underneath.

I forget to breathe for half a second.

I slow down near the fence, trying to look normal. My fingers fumble with the hem of my jacket. Abort mission? Keep running? Say something?

Before I can fully talk myself out of it, I blurt, "Hey... um... you're back."

His movement stills.

Then, slowly, he sits up.

His gaze lands on me. Steady. Sharp. The kind of eyes that make you feel seen—fully, completely, undeniably. I felt naked beneath it.

Then he shifts, lashes dropping low.

*Wait.*

*Hold on.*

*He has ridiculous lashes.*

*Like, the kind that shouldn't belong to a man. Dark. Long. The type that girls spend thousands on extensions trying to get.*

Okay, stop staring. Stop staring.

And then he speaks.

"Morning, ma'am."

I blink.

Ma'am? Excuse me?

A laugh escapes me—awkward, amused. "Okay, first of all, I'm not a 'ma'am'. You can drop that."

There's no expression change, but something shifts. Something small.

"I, uh... noticed you before. Then you vanished."

His gaze flickers for a fraction of a second.

"Had a procedure," he says. "Needed rest."

Minimal words. Maximum impact. Oh god—hide, hide, or run. Or both.

"Right... makes sense."

I shift my weight. Why is my heart hammering like I just sprinted?

"I'm Aarohi, by the way."

A pause. A long pause.

Then, finally: "Lieutenant Commander Arjun."

He offers a brief, firm handshake. His palm is rough and warm.

His gaze flicks over me, assessing, calculating.

I swallow. Fried. My brain is fried.

"Well, um..." I need an exit. "I just... saw you and thought I'd say hi. Hope you recover soon."

A beat.

Then, softer this time: "Thank you."

He reaches for his crutches, and for some reason, I feel a tiny pang of regret.

I nod quickly. "I'll—uh—let you get back to it."

And then I ran away.

What. The. Hell. Was. That?

The cool air rushes past, but my cheeks are burning.

This was nothing. Just a normal, polite interaction.

Except—

Oh damn. I ran.

Like, actually ran.

Not a casual jog. Not a smooth, dignified exit.

I bolted.

Full sprint. No looking back. If only I had this kind of speed during my long runs, I'd have finished a marathon by now.

This is ridiculous.

# Chapter 3: I saw her.

## Arjun

**2:37 AM.**

I stare at the ceiling. Again.

Sleep doesn't come easy these days. It's not just the pain—it's the waiting. Between the dull, persistent ache in my legs and the relentless thoughts in my head, there's no rest. No true stillness.

And yet, everything around me is still.

The hospital is quiet at this hour. A place that's always brimming with movement, orders and footsteps—at night, it slows down. Almost like it's holding its breath.

I shift slightly, trying to find a comfortable position. A useless attempt.

I've been here for weeks. Therapy sessions, assessments, waiting for the next decision. Will I make the medical cut? Will I wear the badge again? Will my body obey me the way it once did?

No answers. Just waiting.

And when you wait long enough, the world outside starts to blur.

People walk in and out of the hospital grounds—officers reporting for duty, families visiting patients, nurses moving between rooms. Life moves fast, but for me, everything has slowed to a painful crawl.

But then, there's her.

**5:45 AM.**

Every morning. Like clockwork.

She cuts across my window view, she runs like she means it, like the world depends on it. Always with a running pouch strapped to her waist. And always, always with food tucked inside for stray dogs.

I wait for that part.

Where she pauses at the edge of the alley to feed the strays— the same four dogs that now wait just for her. They wag their tails before she even bends down.

And then... she does a little happy dance, her ponytail swinging over her head. In that moment, she's so breathtakingly beautiful, it stays with me—playing on a loop in my mind until the next day, when I wait to see her again

It makes me smirk. Just for a second.

I don't know who she is. I don't know why I notice.

But for those brief moments in the morning—

Forget that I can't run.

Forget that I used to.

Forget that I might never again.

# Chapter 4: Black

## Aarohi

### Sunday: The Community Fun Run

**7:00 a.m.** - The crisp morning air crackles with anticipation at the community makeshift starting line. It's a weekly tradition—anyone, from defence personnel, their families to residents, can sign up. I'm tackling a 10K this time, aiming to build stamina for my upcoming half marathon.

"Three...two...one—go!"

We're off. My feet thrum against the pavement. Some surge ahead like seasoned pros, others keep a steady jog in friendly packs, chatting between breaths. I settle into a comfortable rhythm, letting the energy of the crowd propel me forward around neat rows of army quarters and cheering onlookers.

Around 1 hour and 10 minutes later, I push through the final stretch, lungs burning, legs screaming in protest. The bright FINISH banner looms ahead, and with one last effort, I stumble across, gasping for breath. A volunteer steps forward, slipping the finisher's medal over my head.

I drift toward the sideline, hands on my knees as I try to catch my breath. That's when I spotted Sneha, a colonel's daughter I've met a few times at these events. She waves me over, her own medal glinting under the sun.

"Good job!" she says, offering a friendly fist bump. "How'd it go?"

I exhale sharply, still recovering. "Exhausting. But honestly? I think I only keep running for the medal at the end."

Sneha chuckles. "Right? It's the only reward that makes the pain feel worth it." She tilts her head toward the canteen. "Lemonade? You in?"

I'm about to nod when a deep, familiar voice behind me cuts through the noise.

"Good morning."

I turn, heart doing an Olympic-level somersault.

Arjun.

Dressed in his usual all-black workout gear. Either he owns nothing but black—or he's seriously committed to the aesthetic. (And my stupid brain, ever dramatic, wonders: maybe he has a black heart too.)

He stands just a few feet away, leaning on one crutch. His gaze is steady. Unreadable. But there's something in his eyes—just a flicker—that sends a quiet warmth crawling up my spine.

"Oh," I manage, "hi."

He flicks his gaze to the medal. "Congratulations on finishing. How was the run?"

Sneha arches an eyebrow and shifts subtly away, sensing our conversation. "I'll be at the canteen, Aarohi," she says pointedly, then ducks into the crowd.

I clear my throat, cheeks warm. "It was tough but good. I finished around an hour and ten minutes—nothing record-breaking, but hey, medal's a medal," I say, trying for a light tone.

Arjun's lips tug into a faint half-smile. "Beats being at home. Looks like you enjoyed it."

"I did," I admit. "What brings you here? You, um, watching the runs?"

He taps the crutch lightly. "Doctor said I can move around more, so I figured I'd at least show up—get back into the atmosphere. Miss running."

A flicker of sympathy catches me. "I'm sure you'll be back soon," I say gently, noting the frustration etched across his brow. "How's the recovery going?"

"Slower than I'd like," he says, voice controlled. "But better than it was."

I nod, adjusting my medal. "Well, at least you're out and about. That's something."

He glances beyond me, like he's on the verge of leaving, but then hesitates. "So, what're your plans for the rest of the day?" he asks.

I perk up. "Actually, after I shower, I'm heading to Bangla Sahib Gurudwara. I go sometimes on Sundays—I find it peaceful. I love the vibe."

He tilts his head, curiosity sparking in his dark eyes. "I've passed it a few times. Never got the chance to step in."

A silent beat passes. Then Arjun speaks again, voice quieter. "Would it...be okay if I joined you? If it's not too personal."

My heart jolts, a mix of surprise and an odd thrill tightening in my chest. "Oh! Sure," I manage, catching my breath. "If you want to come, absolutely."

He gestures at his crutch. "I'll need to change. Sweat and all. Meet in, say, an hour? Can I have your number... uh, to find you?"

Heat creeps up my cheeks as I take his phone. My fingers brush against his—just a fleeting touch, but it sends a shiver down my spine. I type my number, slower than intended, hesitating for half a second before hitting save. As I enter my name—**Aarohi**—I almost add a smiley emoji at the end but stop myself at the last moment.

"Here it is," I say, forcing a casual smile, though the warmth in my cheeks betrays me. I hand his phone back, trying not to dwell on the way my fingers still tingle.

He nods, the corner of his mouth lifting almost imperceptibly. "See you then, Aarohi."

He turns, moving smoothly despite the crutch, disappearing into the thinning crowd. I stand there for a moment, adrenaline still zinging in my veins. He asked if he could come along.

If Siya were here, she'd smirk. "Here we go, Ms. Hopeless Romantic." She's seen it all—breakups, patch-ups, my grand declarations of love, my sudden exits. I can already hear her teasing me. But I can't help the warmth unfurling in my chest as I head to join Sneha for lemonade.

I sling the door shut behind me as I reach home, tossing my finish medal on the coffee table. My legs still hum from the 10K, and my T-shirt clings to me in a decidedly unappealing way.

In the bathroom, hot water cascades over my shoulders, rinsing away the layer of sweat and dust. My mind replays Arjun's calm "Good morning," and the subtle half-smile he gave me when he said he'd join me at the Gurudwara. *He asked me if he could come along,* I remind myself, still half in disbelief.

*Don't overthink it, Aarohi,* I scold silently, grabbing the body wash. But a twist of excitement keeps me from fully relaxing. Soon enough, I'm out of the shower, hair dripping as I rummage through my wardrobe for something "appropriate but casual."

I finally settle on a simple green suit with a lightweight palazzo. It's modest enough for the Gurudwara and comfortable enough for a Sunday morning outing. I hold it up to my reflection, second-guessing. Am I dressing up too much? Or too little?

A moment's hesitation—and a mental image of Arjun in his classic black—makes me shrug. "This'll do," I mutter. I can't prance in sweaty running gear, and I'm definitely not about to show up in jeans and a T-shirt at Bangla Sahib.

I'm not one for heavy makeup, so I keep it simple: a dab of lightweight foundation for a bit of coverage, the tiniest smudge of lipstick I can also tap onto my cheeks for a hint of blush, and my trusty sunscreen. Eyeliner? I attempt a thin line, quickly deciding it's passable enough not to ruin my entire look. A quick brush through my still-damp hair, leaving it in a loose, low ponytail.

Of course, I can't skip my signature perfume. This one is for days when I need confidence—*top notes of coffee, delicate middle notes of jasmine and tuberose, and grounding base notes of cocoa, vanilla, sandalwood, and tonka bean.* I loved spritzing where my pulse thrummed behind my ears and on my wrists. First, a dab of moisturizer to help the fragrance last, then a quick spray.

"Okay, that's it, this is not a big deal. Just a Gurudwara visit. With a friend. Who also happens to be frustratingly attractive." I tell myself, my pulse thrumming with something between excitement and nerves.

Back in the living room, I snatch my car keys. I check the time on my phone. Forty minutes since we parted ways. I type a quick text to Arjun: *"On my way. See you in ~15?"*

Within seconds, his reply pings: *"See you soon."* A two-word response, but it sends a tiny thrill skittering through me. *Pull it together, Aarohi.*

I think I'm officially breaking every unwritten rule in the Girl Code of Dating. I mean, I approached him first. That alone should've been strike one. You're supposed to dodge a guy at least three times before you even think about saying yes—make him work for it, keep him guessing. But me? One big, eager "yes" flew out of my mouth like it had been rehearsed.

And don't even get me started on the rest.

There's a whole ritual, right? You're supposed to wait five or six dates—minimum—before sex even crosses your mind. Keep the mystery alive, slow burn, build the tension. But the way I'm moving with him? The way my eyes practically drink him in every time he's near. The way my body betrays me, leaning toward him, reacting before my brain catches up?

It's like I've hit fast-forward on everything. Emotional connection? Check. Physical chemistry? Double-check. And I can't even pretend to play it cool. I'm not being chill—I'm being completely, unapologetically swept up.

Too fast. Too intense. Too... real.

But also? It feels way too good to stop.

# Chapter 5: Of Dreams and Scars

## Aarohi

The drive is mercifully short—a realization that makes me wonder how close we actually live. I pull into the same parking area near the regiment's sports complex, scanning for Arjun. My pulse flutters when I spot him leaning against a low wall, still relying on his single crutch, but looking far more put-together than before: a blue button-up shirt, dark jeans, and casual sneakers.

*Oh? A splash of color? Maybe his wardrobe isn't entirely black after all.*

I hop out, smoothing the front of my suit. His gaze flicks over me—not lingering too long, but enough to send warmth rising up my neck.

"Hey," I say, stepping closer. "You clean up well."

He gives a small, acknowledging nod. "So do you. Green suits you." His voice remains low and calm, but there's a flicker in his eyes that suggests genuine appreciation.

Enough to make every nerve in my body buzz to life, as if even the tiniest hair follicles suddenly wake up. Internally, I've taken a victory lap around the world.

I shift my keys to my other hand. "Should we take my car? Or yours?"

He pats his crutch lightly. "Walking long distances is still tricky. If you're okay to drive, that'd be better."

"Sure," I reply, unlocking the car. For a beat, we both stand there, a curious silence stretching between us. My heart picks up speed again—

Finally, I wave toward the passenger seat. "Get in." Then mentally cringe. *Who even says that, Aarohi?*

"Sounds good," he says, carefully manoeuvring himself into the seat. I circle around to the driver's side, sliding in and starting the engine. As I pull away from the curb, I throw him a quick smile. "Ever been inside a Gurdwara before?"

He shakes his head. "No. I've passed by, but never went in."

"Well, time for a first," I say, trying to keep my tone light. My stomach flips again—a swirl of excitement and nerves. Because whatever this is—just a shared outing, or something more—I can't deny that it feels good to have him here, sitting next to me.

A soft 90s Bollywood song plays quietly in the background—something mellow and romantic, maybe *Pehla Nasha*, low enough not to dominate the conversation.

He breaks the comfortable silence first. "You often visit Gurdwaras, or is this a rare Sunday thing?"

I let out a small laugh. "Oh, I'm a regular. I'm not Sikh," I clarify. "But I believe in Ek Onkar—God is one. I find absolute peace at Gurdwaras." I gesture vaguely with one hand. "Wherever the energy resonates with you, that's your place, you know?"

He tips his head, intrigued. "Energy!"

"Exactly," I say, nodding enthusiastically. "I'm kind of big on visualization—not the write-it-100-times kind—more like picturing the end result, letting that vision guide your actions so the universe lines up all the right pieces."

Arjun exhales, a hint of amusement in his eyes. "So, you visualize, and everything falls into place."

A playful grin spreads across my face. "Well, not magically. I work hard, too. But I think manifestation is about aligning your internal belief with your outer efforts. When you have that clarity—poof! The path unravels." I pause, catching myself talking a bit too fast. "And Gurdwaras taught me about giving back. Like Seva—selfless service. The more you give, the more you realize how blessed you actually are. Gratitude amplifies blessings."

He watches me a second longer than I expect. "You're...very passionate."

He nods, letting my words sink in. "So, when you're not running what do you do, Aarohi?

A giggle slips out. "I work at Evora Events—I'm a Project Manager for event registrations and stuff. But that's not my real dream."

He raises an eyebrow. "So, what's the real dream?"

My cheeks warm with excitement. "I'm building my own perfume brand—Nocturnal Essence. It's still very small, like tiny, basically me in my makeshift lab at home." I gesture at the dashboard, reaching over to pop open the glove compartment. "In fact, I have a prototype right here. No fancy label yet—just my initial formula."

I carefully hand him a small glass bottle. Its clear liquid glints in the morning light. "It's a woman's perfume," I warn, "but you can give it a sniff if you like."

Arjun unscrews the cap, dabs a little on his wrist, then inhales. "Hmm. Vanilla?"

And amber, with a touch of woody undertones," I say, grinning. "Took me a few trials to get those layers right. I wanted something warm, comforting—like freshly baked cookies."

I pause, suddenly feeling a little ridiculous. "Okay, this is embarrassing, but the idea actually came from a scene in a movie I saw as a kid. There's this aunt who tells her niece: 'Always bake something when a guy comes over—cookies, croissants, anything—so that whenever he passes by any bakery and his nostrils hit the similar notes, he'll think of you. That's what fragrances do to you—they turn into memories."

I shake my head, laughing at myself. "So, my vision? To bottle that feeling. That freshly baked, roasted-vanilla warmth—except in a perfume instead of an oven."

I snort at my own story.

He brings his wrist up again, takes another whiff, and gives me a sideways glance.

"Careful," he says, voice low, teasing. "If your plan was to make someone think of you every time they pass a bakery... it's definitely working."

My breath catches.

He regards the bottle with newfound respect. "That's...pretty creative," he admits. "So, eventually you want to launch this full scale?"

"Oh, yeah," I exhale dreamily. "I want to craft my formula from scratch, bottle design and all. My big vision is to build a standalone brand. But for now, I'm learning, saving up, and perfecting blends one test bottle at a time."

Arjun tucks the perfume back in the glove compartment with care. "Impressive."

A flush of pride warms my chest. "Thanks. It's a long road, but I'm patient."

The 90s song fades into another soft tune, and for a moment, we ride in companionable silence. But there's enough electricity in the air to make every hair follicle stand at attention.

I always talk too fast when I'm nervous—but now, in the quiet, my brain is spiraling for me.

I tell myself to focus on the road, but my side-eye betrays me.

I catch the vein in his forearm, the way his shirt hugs his bicep like it was made to torture me.

It's stacked. Toned. Distracting.

And his fingers—long, steady, maddeningly graceful—rest right there by his thigh.

My driving-side view is giving me the most unfair, perfect angle of his hand.

I reach for the gear shift, and my fingers brush against his thigh. Light. Accidental. Electric.

He doesn't flinch. Doesn't move.

And I? I pretend it's nothing. Like I didn't just short-circuit.

Like something between my legs isn't screaming for a reset.

I keep my eyes on the road, nodding along to the music like I'm not absolutely combusting inside.

He shifts slightly in his seat, eyes still fixed ahead—but his voice cuts through the tension, low and casual.

"You always drive this... focused?"

My heart nearly launches into orbit.

I glance at him, trying to keep my tone breezy. "Focused's good. Prevents accidents."

He nods, a faint smirk tugging at the corner of his mouth. "Right. Just... looked like you were about to crush the steering wheel there for a second."

I let out a nervous laugh, willing my hands to relax their death grip. "Guess I'm just... passionate about safe driving."

"And you always change gears that slow... or is this a special performance?"

My heart does a full somersault. I blink. Did he just—?

I force a laugh, gripping the wheel tighter. "That was definitely unintentional."

He hums, low and amused. "Hmm. Seemed pretty... deliberate from where I'm sitting."

I glance at him, flustered, heat crawling up my neck. "Well, maybe *your* thigh shouldn't be loitering so close to my gearshift."

He finally turns, that half-smile playing on his lips—the kind that could ruin lives. "Duly noted. But just so you know..."

His voice dips slightly.

"I didn't mind."

Oh.

Oh *God*.

My insides twist. My fingers twitch. And suddenly, driving in a straight line feels like an Olympic-level challenge.

I bite my lip, eyes on the road, praying for a red light so I can just breathe.

Because he felt it.

He *liked* it.

And now I'm one mildly flirtatious sentence away from pulling over and questioning all my life choices.

---

The golden dome of Bangla Sahib Gurdwara comes into view, glinting in the sunlight. The parking lot is bustling with cars and people, families in all colours attired hurrying inside. I find a spot, turn off the ignition, and exhale finally.

"Well, we're here," I announce softly, a hint of reverence creeping into my voice. We step out, and a mild breeze swirls around us. I grab my dupatta, draping it over my head to cover my hair. He takes a light scarf from his pocket, tying it around his head with a focused expression. A sense of calm envelops me as we make our way to the shoe counter, where we slip off our footwear and hand them over with grateful smiles. The fragrance of prasad wafts through the air, mingling with the soft hum of kirtan from within. My heart feels lighter, as it always does here.

Arjun matches my pace, crutch in hand but moving steadily. "So, this is it," he murmurs, scanning the surroundings. I nod, voice lowered in respect. "Let's go in. I'll show you how the seating works, then we can just...maybe sit for a while, absorb the peace." He gives me a small, genuine smile. We started to climb the steps together—

The white marble steps leading into Bangla Sahib Gurdwara glimmer under the soft morning sun. The distant hum of kirtan drifts through the air, and I feel the usual warmth seeping into my chest—the kind of peace I only find here. Arjun matches his pace to his single crutch, but I notice how slowly he's forced to move. I try to walk just a little slower—casually—so he won't sense I'm accommodating him. To our right, I noticed the familiar line snaking around the corner—devotees waiting for the morning langar. Some barefoot, some clutching empty steel thalis. Just beyond that, another queue was forming outside the Gurdwara's free medical wing. Mothers holding children wrapped in shawls, elderly men sitting on low steps, rubbing their knees. I watched in silence for a few seconds—the way hope and hardship stood shoulder to shoulder. Hunger, illness, fatigue... everything stripped bare under the morning sky. "There's so much pain in the world. So much to ask from God, so much to pray for," I whispered, my voice barely above the hum of the kirtan.

Arjun followed my gaze and whispered in a low voice "You know, sometimes people don't pray for healing. Or for miracles." I turned slightly toward him. "Sometimes," he said, eyes fixed on the crowd ahead, "they just pray to see the dead body of their loved one. So, they can say a final goodbye."

My breath caught in my chest.

He looked away from me then, like the memory had grabbed him by the collar and dragged him back.

We stop at the threshold. I press my forehead to the floor to bow down, but out of the corner of my eye, I see Arjun struggle, his jaw clenching. He's trying to bend, but his left leg won't cooperate. He finally settles for a deep squat, bowing his head low. A pang zips through me.

He straightens slowly, gripping his crutch. We step inside, following the stream of visitors around the holy water tank— the sacred Sarovar. People traditionally sprinkle a few drops of water on themselves, a symbolic cleansing. We move in a slow circle around the water, the low murmur of prayers resonating all around us. After a few quiet moments, I glance at him and ask, softly, "Earlier... you said something about how people sometimes just pray to see the dead body of someone they love. What did you mean?"

He exhales slowly, his gaze drifting across the calm surface of the Sarovar.

"I'm a clearance diver. Part of a special forces cadre in the Navy," he begins quietly.

"About ten, eleven months ago, my team and I were sent to Manipur. A dam had breached, water swept through an entire village, including a football field where kids were playing."

His voice tightens. "We thought it was going to be a rescue op. But... it turned into a retrieval. We had to pull the bodies of those kids out from nets, from under the rubble. Their families were standing there, waiting, praying endlessly. Not eating. Not sleeping. Just waiting—to perform the last rites. To say goodbye."

A knot rises in my throat at the image.

I hesitate, but the question sits heavy on my tongue. "If you don't mind... Can I ask what happened?" I glance at his legs, hoping he understands.

He nods slightly, then continues. "After that operation, I needed a break. One of my coursemates from NDA was getting married. I thought a few days away might help clear my head..."

He swallows hard, pausing to steady himself. We edge a bit further, careful not to block the path of other devotees. "It was really cold and foggy. We rode out on his bike—he drove, I rode pillion. Next thing I know, we've hit something. The bike skids, I'm on the road, my friend's thrown a few feet away, but he's conscious, just scraped up. And me...my leg was pinned under the bike, twisted in ways it shouldn't twist. Blood everywhere." He gestures briefly at his legs. "I woke up in the hospital. My friend ended up getting married the very next day, with minimal injuries. Me? Not so lucky."

I spot the tremor in his jaw, the tension in his shoulders. "Multiple surgeries, both legs messed up," he explains. "And because the accident happened while I was on leave, not on duty, it's considered...my own responsibility, in a way. I've got twelve months to recover enough to get back to clearance diving. Otherwise, I'll be out."

A soft "Oh" escapes me. My heart clenches. I can't help but picture the countless hours of training he must have endured to be part of special forces—and how precarious it all seems now. "So that's why you push yourself so hard every morning," I say gently. "I see you doing those crunches, running exercises with crutches..."

He nods, expression grim. "Yeah. I'm hoping for a miracle, to be honest. I need to pass the fitness criteria again, or it's over."

I bite my lip. A flicker of empathy spurs me to say something comforting. "I'm sure you'll make it. But even if—just in case—things go differently, maybe there's a bigger plan for you, something better than you can imagine right now."

His lips press into a firm line. "I don't believe in a Plan B," he admits, voice low. "Sometimes, the only good plan is the one you're already on."

I realize my well-intended encouragement has fallen flat. He doesn't want a 'maybe there's something else' talk. He wants his life back. "Right," I murmur, nodding. "I get it."

We continue the slow walk around the Sarovar, quiet and pensive. At one point, I glance over and see the anguish still etched on his face. Something tugs inside my chest—an urge to somehow protect him, or help him, though I barely know him. Why am I so invested? Gently turning my eyes toward the main prayer hall—"Please...bless him"—I find myself praying silently, folding my hands at the threshold.

Not long after, we make our way out, retrieving our shoes. The hush that envelopes Arjun feels...heavier than the peaceful silence we found inside. The bustle of traffic and voices are a stark contrast to the calm we just experienced. He settles into the passenger seat again, carefully placing his crutch at his feet. I start the engine, and we pull away. For half the ride, neither of us speaks. It's not uncomfortable, exactly—more like there's a weight in the air, the echoes of his story hanging between us.

Eventually, the single officers' quarters where he's staying come into view, set behind a high wall and guarded gate. He points for me to stop. I do, stepping on the brake more gently than usual. "Thank you," he says quietly, unbuckling his seatbelt. The earlier spark in his voice—when we talked about perfumes and manifestation—has dulled under the memory of his trauma.

I hesitate, wanting to say something reassuring, something that'll mend that heartbreak I glimpsed. But words fail me. All I manage is a soft "Take care." He grabs his crutch, pushing the car door open.

Before climbing out, he pauses, eyes lingering on me for a moment. There's gratitude there—and also lingering sadness. "I appreciate it, Aarohi," he says, voice steady despite the emotion. Then, with measured effort, he maneuvers himself upright and closes the door.

I watch him head toward the building, the crutch tapping against the pavement in a slow, methodical rhythm. A tightness grips my chest—part empathy, part helplessness. I barely know this man, yet I feel a fierce pang of concern for him.

My fingers grip the steering wheel. Why do I feel like crying?

A breath shudders out of me as I drive away, the heaviness following me like a cloud. There's a swirl of emotions I can't fully name.

I take out my phone, open Arjun's chat and send him a text: *"When life feels unfair, just do an act of kindness. It might help you see the world a little differently."*

# Chapter 6: Craving

## Aarohi

**8:37 PM**

My phone screen lights up.

**Arjun:** You up?

I stare at his name. I shift under my blanket, my hair still damp from the shower, curled up in my oversized T-shirt. My fingers hover over the keyboard.

Do I answer immediately? No.

Do I want to answer? Yes.

So, I wait. Exactly two minutes.

**Me:** Barely. Why?

A pause.

**Arjun:** You eat?

I frown at the screen, and right on cue, my stomach growls. Betrayal. *Damn him*—for always asking the right questions.

**Me:** Uhh... had a cup of chai. That counts, right?

**Arjun:** Not unless you're five years old.

**Me:** Five-year-olds don't drink chai.

**Arjun:** Meet me at Zephyr. I'm craving food—and your company, if you're up for it.

I stare at the message, my brows pulling together. A small flutter kicks up in my stomach.

**Me:** What if I don't want to?

**Arjun:** Then I'll be eating delicious dal makhani all by myself, and you'll be sitting in your room, hungry.

I exhale, tossing my blanket off.

**Me:** Fine.

**Arjun:** Done. See you in 15.

I stare at my reflection in the mirror, biting my lip. Fifteen minutes.

Ugh. Why am I suddenly overthinking what to wear?

It's just dinner.

Just. Dinner.

Zephyr is a dinner place inside the naval component, and I've never been there before. But I know that any restaurant inside a defence area means strict dress codes. Men need collared shirts, tucked-in pants, and formal shoes. Women? They can wear anything as long as it's modest.

I pull on a soft knit sweater and my best-fitted jeans, ruffling my damp hair to give it some volume. A dash of perfume, just because.

Grabbing my keys, I check myself one last time in the mirror. Casual, but cute.

## Zephyr – 9:10 PM

The restaurant has a quiet elegance to it—warm lights, polished wooden interiors, the faint hum of conversations around neatly arranged tables and live music playing softly in the corner, mostly instrumental. I spot Arjun instantly, sitting near the window, effortlessly at ease.

He's in a dark blue polo, sleeves pushed up to his forearms. The veins in his arms make my stomach do circles. His watch gleams under the light as he checks the time.

He looks up, spots me, and gives a small, knowing smirk.

I roll my eyes but walk toward him, my heart doing something I don't want to acknowledge.

"Hey," I say, sliding into the chair across from him.

"Hey," he replies, handing me a menu. "Ordered for you already."

I raise an eyebrow. "Confident."

He leans back in his chair. "Efficient."

A waiter arrives, placing two steaming bowls of dal makhani and butter naan in front of us. My stomach instantly approves.

"Not bad," I murmur.

Arjun chuckles. "I wasn't sure what you'd like to drink, so I left that part for you to decide."

I instantly reply, "A glass of white wine would be perfect."

He asks, "Chardonnay, okay?"

I nod, "Hmm, yes!"

He calls the waiter and asks for the glass of Chardonnay.

I ask, "You won't drink?"

He says softly, "I'm in recovery currently, so I'm avoiding alcohol completely."

I instantly feel embarrassed. "Oh, I didn't mean to drink alone—"

But he assures me, smiling gently, "Hey, it's okay."

Looking at Arjun, you'd never guess there were rods holding his legs together. He carries himself like nothing ever broke. His persona doesn't even make you feel he's hurting. The charm, composure, and build of his body—suddenly, I'm imagining what it would feel like to hug him. Literally, I would be completely hidden in his arms.

I dig in, letting the rich, buttery taste melt in my mouth. He watches me with a knowing glint in his eyes.

"So," he says, looking directly at me. "What exactly do you want, Aarohi?"

For a second, I feel caught—as if he were reading my mind. I never want him to know what goes through my mind when I see him. I look up, licking butter off my fingers. "In life?"

He nods.

"Oh," I exhale, tucking a loose strand of hair behind my ear. "A lot. I have a hundred plans—launching Nocturnal Essence, my own perfume brand. Running marathons. Skydiving in Dubai. Mountaineering in the Himalayas…"

His lips twitch into a half-smile. "And I'm sure you will do it all", and his leg slightly brushed against mine under the table.

I freeze. Just for a second. Every nerve in my body suddenly tunes in.

To bring back control of my body, I changed the topic to "I have a meeting with a vendor for fragrance oils & a bottle manufacturer in Kannauj, UP, next month."

Arjun tilts his head. "Kannauj?"

I nod, excitement bubbling. "It's the perfume city of India. Perfume-making there goes back to the Mughal era. They still prepare fragrances traditionally. I learned perfumery there."

Arjun watches me, then leans forward, resting his forearms on the table. "Mind if I come along?"

I blink. "What?"

"I'm free this weekend," he says, as if it's the most normal thing in the world.

For a second, I don't know what to say. He wants to come. With me?

I hesitate but then nod slowly. "Okay. You can come."

There's a pause, but his presence crackles around me. I feel every inch of it—like static on skin.

I don't know if I'm blushing, but I feel hot.

I reach for my wine glass, sipping too quickly just to keep my hands busy. Anything to anchor myself.

**9:40 PM**

Arjun watches me, amused. "How's running going?"

I relax a little, grateful for the change in topic. "Good. I'm preparing for a marathon. Haven't decided which one, but this year—I want to do it."

He nods, taking a sip of his drink. "And after that? What's the big goal?"

I grin. "Maybe an Ironman someday." I laugh, clearly joking.

He lifts an eyebrow. "Ironman—or Ironwoman in your case? That's awesome."

He doesn't laugh. Of course, for him, it's not a joke.

Look at him. He could do it tomorrow if he wanted.

He shrugged, a bemused smile tugging at his lips. "You'd have to train relentlessly for it."

I felt a twinge of embarrassment as I admitted, "Well...I don't exactly know how to swim, so Ironman isn't happening anytime soon in my life."

His eyebrows shot up. "Wait, you don't swim? You're always talking about taking on the world. I just assumed you could do anything."

I shrugged, staring at my fingers. "I tried once, in eighth or ninth grade. But I quit after a few days because..."

Arjun's gaze softened. "Because what?"

A mixture of shame and old hurt uncoiled in my chest. I cleared my throat and began, "It was during the summer holidays, and I'd started lessons at a pool near our house. My mom's big on trying new things—she convinced me to sign up. I loved it...until I got really tanned. I mean, my skin went multiple shades darker. And I know it sounds shallow, but in North India, people talk. A lot. Especially about skin color."

"One afternoon, I was sitting on my bed, hair wet, flipping through a book, when my dad passed by. He stopped, took a couple of steps back, and joked, 'Aarohi, your hair colour is almost blending with your face now. What's going on?' He laughed about it, told me to wear sunscreen. He meant no harm, but..."

I exhaled, remembering the hollow feeling in my chest that day. "I know he wasn't insulting me. But it hit hard. A few days later, at a family gathering, he made a similar joke about my mom's complexion. Everyone laughed, like it was normal. Mom's face tightened. She pretended it didn't matter, but I could see how much it stung. And I just...didn't know how to defend her or myself. I was a kid."

I tried to sound casual, but old insecurities hovered at the edge of my words. "After that, I was too embarrassed. I quit swimming so I wouldn't tan even more. I started thinking, maybe I'm not cut out for these things."

A quiet settled between us. The din of the café around us— clinking cups, low chatter—suddenly felt distant.

Arjun leaned back in his seat. "You know," he began gently, "tan lines fade. If you stayed out of the sun for a week or two, your skin colour would even out again. But that skill you'd have gained—swimming—that would stick with you forever. It's not just for fun; it could save your life someday. You love experiences, right? Why let a little sunlight keep you from something that could open up an entire world of adventure?"

He leaned closer, his voice low. "Seriously. A bit of tan? That's a small price for seeing coral reefs while scuba diving or finishing an Iron—sorry, Ironwoman—race," he said with a teasing wink. "Everything you do, all those experiences—they shape who you are more than any fleeting change in skin tone."

For a moment, I simply stared at him. "You've got a point."

He reached across the table and placed a hand over mine. "Well!"

Finally, I breathed out. "You're right."

Arjun smirked. "Then start by letting me teach you."

A flash of surprise lit my eyes.

"I'd love that," I whispered, meaning every syllable.

I wasn't thrilled about spilling my insecurities like that—not to someone I barely know.

Usually, I like to keep it together. Show people I've got it all figured out.

But with him... it's like the rawest parts of me just keep slipping out.

And even though my heart feels safe, my mind is telling me to be cautious.

# Chapter 6.5: Something About Her

## Arjun

I wanted to touch her.

To pull her close.

To feel her mouth against mine.

To bury my fingers in her hair and kiss her like I've been starving for it.

Because I am.

But I didn't.

She just looked too delicate in that moment—like sunlight caught in glass. And I'm afraid if I reach for her the way I want to, I'll shatter her.

So, I stood there, hands clenched in my pockets, pretending I wasn't unraveling.

Pretending I hadn't memorized the way her lips curved when she smiled... or the way her eyes flicked down to my mouth, just for a second, like maybe she wanted the same thing.

And then she said goodbye.

Softly.

And I watched her drive away, wondering how someone so light could make all this weight inside me feel a little easier to carry.

She has no idea how beautiful she is.

Not in the way the world measures it.

But in the way her eyes carry the weight of a thousand feelings she never says out loud.

You can see her soul in them—like glass.

Compassion. Kindness. Chaos.

They shimmer with unshed tears even when she's trying to act unfazed.

As if the world moves her just a little more deeply than it should.

She walks like she doesn't know people are watching.

Like her body isn't poetry in motion.

Like that soft curve of her waist, the wild looseness of her hair, the way she tilts her head when she's curious—aren't enough to bring a man to his knees.

She's sexy without trying.

Without realizing that the way her sweater clings, or how she tucks her hair behind her ear mid-conversation, makes it nearly impossible to look away.

And when she gets nervous—or shy—she bites her lip.

Soft. Quick. Like she doesn't even know she's doing it.

And God... she has no idea how hard I have to work to control my urge to lean in.

She laughs—unguarded, a little loud—and I swear, I forget every single reason I've ever had to keep my distance.

She tries to carry this image of being strong.

And she is.

But underneath it all... she's just a girl. A little girl who's been told to be more. Do more.

Hold it together.

And I don't know if I have the right to be near something that delicate.

Something that good.

Because I'm not whole.

I'm still picking up the wreckage. Still swallowing parts of me I don't want anyone to see.

Some days I feel like a half-man—quietly drowning in my own silence.

And yet...

I can't stay away from her.

She makes things feel quieter. Lighter. Like maybe this ache doesn't have to last forever.

She's all heart—even when she pretends, she isn't.

And being around her makes me want to try harder.

I don't know what this is between us.

But I know this:

She's the first person I've looked at and thought—

*Please, don't let me break her.*

## Chapter 7:

*He didn't arrive like a storm.*

*He arrived like the stillness after—and somehow, that ruined me more.*

## Aarohi

The clock on my laptop read 5:32 p.m. I stretched my neck from side to side, trying to ease the tension that had built up after hours of working. For days, I'd been creating an event registration website for a client's upcoming cruise event—tweaking the site design, building custom forms, and making sure the user experience was seamless.

It was nearly the end of the workday, but I still had a few final checks to run. My phone buzzed with a text message:

**Arjun:** "Hey, if free, meet me downstairs in 30?"

I blinked at my screen. *Huh?*

**Me:** *Downstairs? Where?*

**Arjun:** *Your office building. Where else?*

My fingers hovered over the keyboard, my heart doing something stupidly unnecessary.

**Me:** *Wait—what? What are you doing here?*

**Arjun:** *Okay, Google Maps works. I know where your office is, Aarohi.*

I huffed out a small laugh, shaking my head. *Of course, he does.*

**Me:** *So, you just... showed up?*

**Arjun:** *Yes*

A rush of excitement fluttered in my stomach. Since when has my life become this flurry of heart-thudding texts and after-work meetups? I texted back a quick reply— "Give me 15 mins!"—then scrambled to finalize the last pieces of the registration page.

Finally, with a satisfied sigh, I shut my laptop. I grabbed my purse, hurried to the restroom, and surveyed myself in the mirror: I was wearing a charcoal-grey bodycon dress that hugged my curves in a way that made me feel both fierce and a little self-conscious. Perfect. On my feet were my favourite stilettos, giving me that extra inch of confidence (plus a slight pinch in my toes, but I'd survive).

By 5:50 p.m., I was in the elevator, heart pounding. When I reached the ground-floor cafeteria, I spotted Arjun almost instantly. He stood near a table by the window, wearing a casual grey T-shirt and jeans—simple, but somehow exuding effortless confidence. A small paper bag lay on the table next to two steaming cups of coffee.

He caught my eye and gave me a soft smile. I walked over, my stilettos clicking on the tiled floor. We did our usual side hug—slightly awkward, but sweet. His arm felt warm around my shoulders.

"Hey," I said, breathless for no good reason.

"Hey," he replied, handing me a cup of coffee. "Figured you might need a pick-me-up."

I sipped, grateful for the caffeine and the momentary distraction. "Thanks. So, what's in the bag?"

He gave me a slight smirk. "Something for you. But before you say anything, no—it's not a gift."

Curiosity piqued; I peeked into the brown paper bag. My eyes went wide when I saw a navy-blue swimsuit, cut in a style that was both modest and flattering—a little skirt around the hips, adjustable straps at the top. My cheeks heated, and my stomach flipped with a mix of delight and nerves.

"You, uh...you bought me a swimsuit?" My voice came out a little higher than intended.

Arjun nodded, entirely matter-of-factly. "Swimming lessons start on Sunday. Six a.m. sharp. I told you I'd teach you. Now you have the right gear."

My heart practically cartwheeled in my chest. I stared at it, blinking. "But...you got my size exactly right!"

He shrugged, that faint smile still dancing around his lips. "I pay attention."

I couldn't decide if I wanted to squeal or hide under the table. Silence stretched between us, but it was comfortable. My gaze flickered to the swimsuit in the bag. Just hours ago, I was in full work mode. Now, here I was, holding a reminder that soon I'd be stepping out of my comfort zone—literally plunging into a pool.

Arjun's phone buzzed, and he glanced at it, grimacing a bit. "I should let you go."

I nodded, slipping the swimsuit bag into my tote. "Yeah, thanks for the coffee. And...this," I added, lifting the bag slightly.

He stood and offered me a small side hug again, this time lingering just a moment longer. "Sunday. Six a.m. Don't stand me up."

I grinned. "Wouldn't dream of it."

As we parted ways, I felt the teasing weight of the swimsuit in my bag. A swirl of emotions—nerves, excitement, anticipation—followed me out.

# Chapter 8:

*He didn't touch me, but my whole body remembered the traces of him anyway.*

## Aarohi

5:00 a.m., Sunday morning. My alarm rang, but I'd been half-awake for hours already, the buzz of excitement (and nerves) ricocheting inside me. Last night, I bought a cute matching swim cap and goggles, shaved my legs until they were silky-smooth, and then moisturized them before slipping on socks. Now, I hopped into my car feeling strangely giddy.

The sky was still a dark, inky blue by the time I pulled into the parking lot near the base swimming pool. Streetlights cast a warm glow on the pavement. Arjun stood by his car, arms folded over a light hoodie, his breath visible in the chilly morning air.

My stomach flipped at the sight of him. I parked, grabbed my swim bag, and hopped out. He offered a nod and that quiet, self-assured smile.

"Morning," he said, voice low. "Locker rooms are down that path. See you at poolside."

Inside the women's changing area, I slipped into the navy-blue swimsuit he'd given me—still marvelling at how perfectly it fit. The little skirt around the hips added a dash of cuteness. I glanced in the mirror, turning side to side. *You've got this, Aarohi,* I told myself, arms hugging my waist in a quick gesture of self-encouragement. A spritz of my secret body mist was my final flourish. Then I tugged my cap over my hair, goggles perched on top of my head until I needed them.

I took a quick rinse in the shower, squealing softly at how chilly it felt, biting my lip nervously.

When I stepped onto the pool deck, there he was—in the water already, bare-chested, arms braced on the edge. Even across the distance, I could see his muscles and the taut lines of his shoulders. My cheeks instantly flamed. I lowered myself slowly into the water, letting the shock of cold envelop my legs.

He extended a hand to steady me, and I grasped it, grateful. The pool water sent goosebumps up my arms, but I wasn't sure if it was just the temperature or the fact that his fingertips were warm against mine.

"You okay?" he asked, voice echoing slightly in the still morning air.

I nodded. "I'm fine—just...cold." And maybe a bit starstruck by his physique, but I kept that to myself.

He gave a teasing grin. "Don't worry. You'll warm up once you start moving. Ready?"

I forced a laugh, trying to settle my nerves. "Sure. Although, full disclosure—I can only swim if I know I can stand. Depth freaks me out."

Arjun's brow furrowed. "So... you can freestyle, but only if it's shallow enough for you to touch the bottom. That's not really swimming, is it?"

"Hey!" I protested, half embarrassed. "I can float on my back, kind of. And paddle around. I just—if it gets deeper, I panic about getting tired...or drowning."

He shook his head with a sympathetic sigh. "Alright, let's work on that. Actually, the best way to conquer your fear of depth might be to face it."

My eyes went wide. "No, no, no. Let's start gently, okay?"

He laughed softly. "Fine. We'll stay by the rails." He gestured toward the edge of the pool. "You'll swim a few meters holding onto the rail for security, and I'll be right next to you. If you need to rest, just grab the side."

We waded to a shallower section where I could stand comfortably. My heart hammered in my chest—not just from anticipation, but from the closeness. Arjun's body radiated warmth beside me. The moment his gaze flicked over my swimsuit, I pretended not to notice how his gaze lingered.

"Looks good on you," he said quietly.

I couldn't stop my shy smile. "Thanks. Great choice. Really...thank you for, well, all of this."

He shrugged as though it was no big deal. "You can thank me once you're swimming laps without fear."

We started out simple. I pushed off the pool wall and let my arms go into a shaky freestyle. The water parted around my shoulders, and every so often, I'd lift my head to check how far I'd gone. After about ten meters, I paused, clinging to the edge and gulping air. Arjun drifted right behind me—so close I could sense his breath near my ear.

"You're tensing your shoulders," he murmured. "Try to relax. Let the water carry you."

I nodded, still catching my breath. His proximity made my heartbeat do wild flips, and the scent of chlorine mixed with the faint trace of his body wash—clean yet undeniably enticing.

"How's your leg feeling?" I asked, glancing down at where he'd been bandaged weeks ago. "Does swimming help?"

"Yeah. It's easier than running," he said. "In the water, the weights are off my knee and ankles, so I can move around with less pain. It's good rehab."

"That's great," I breathed, truly relieved for him.

He gave me a small half-smile. "Now, no more stalling. Let's go again."

Taking a shaky breath, I pushed off from the wall and kicked as best I could, arms slicing through the water. This time, my form felt a bit smoother—my muscles less rigid. Still, after a few strokes, a wave of nerves washed over me. My mind screamed—what if you sink? I stalled, swallowing an irrational surge of panic, and grabbed for the rail.

"I'm right here," Arjun reminded me, gliding up next to me with powerful strokes. "You're not sinking."

Something about the surety in his voice, the calm steadiness of his presence, gave me courage. I let go of the rail, feeling the flutter of adrenaline in my stomach. Slowly, I started freestyling again, each breath a little deeper, each movement more confident.

When at last I reached the other end of the pool—okay, it wasn't that far, but it felt like miles—I gripped the edge and turned to face him. My lungs burned, but I felt this surprising rush of triumph.

He was close enough that droplets of water from his hair beaded on my shoulder. My gaze flicked over his face, admiring the focus in his eyes.

"See?" he said softly, voice echoing in the early morning quiet. "You can do it."

I nodded, breathless—and not just from the swim. "Yeah. I guess I can."

For a moment, neither of us moved, the water lapping gently around our chests. My heart thundered, he leaned in slightly, as if to say something else, but then the spell broke. A rowdy group of fellow swimmers entered at the far end, their voices echoing off the water. Arjun coughed, flicking his gaze away. "Ready for round two?"

I let out a shaky laugh. "Yep. Let's do it."

# Chapter 9:

*Sometimes, it's not the people you plan with who change your life—it's the ones you didn't see coming.*

## Aarohi

The locker-room mirror was fogged up from the steamy showers. I wiped it clean, glancing at myself once more. I'd quickly changed into a summery, floral knee-length dress, paired with favourite white sneakers, comfortable, and yes, maybe just a little cute.

Stepping outside, the sunlight hit me, warming my skin and sending a shiver down my spine. Or was it seeing Arjun leaning casually against his car? The sleeves of his T-shirt hugged his biceps, muscles that had already distracted me far too much in the pool. He noticed me, eyes twinkling in appreciation, a smile tugging at his lips as his gaze lingered just a moment longer than usual.

I felt my cheeks heat and quickly glanced away, embarrassed that he'd caught me staring too.

But before I could think of something playful or witty to say, my eyes shifted to a figure approaching us from across the parking lot. A tall guy—taller than Arjun, broader around the shoulders but leaner somehow—was walking toward us with a casual, self-assured stride. My brows furrowed, curiosity kicking in when I noticed how similar his face looked to Arjun's. Same sharp jawline, same strong features, and a familiar warmth behind his easy smile.

Arjun turned, following my gaze, and his eyes lit up instantly. "Abhay?"

The man broke into a grin. "Bhai," he said warmly, stretching his arms out for a hug. They clasped each other tightly, the kind of affectionate but firm.

My curiosity stirred. Bhai?

When they pulled back, Arjun turned toward me, his face lighting up with an easy, proud smile. "Aarohi, meet—my younger brother, Major Abhay, a psychiatrist currently serving in the Indian Army." My eyebrows lifted, surprise flickering through me.

"Abhay," Arjun continued, smiling gently at me now, "meet Aarohi."

Abhay stepped forward, extending his hand with an easy, welcoming grin. "Hey, Aarohi. Good to meet you finally. Bhai's talked a lot about you."

I shot Arjun a teasing glance, shaking Abhay's hand firmly. "Has he, now?"

Arjun cleared his throat, looking away slightly, clearly embarrassed at being caught out.

Abhay laughed softly. "Don't worry, all good things. So, how was the swim lesson?"

I laughed, cheeks warming. "Let's just say it was a start. Your brother has a lot of patience."

Arjun rolled his eyes affectionately. "She did great for a beginner."

Abhay chuckled, looking between the two of us with amused eyes. "I'm sure she did."

Unable to resist my curiosity, I tilted my head slightly. "So, both of you joined the defence services?"

Abhay nodded modestly. "Yep, runs in the family, I suppose. Though honestly, Bhai set the bar quite high. I was practicing psychiatry after completing my MBBS, but Bhai inspired me to join."

I laughed softly, my eyes shifting between them, noting their resemblance even more now—the sharpness of their features, the strong jawlines. My thoughts suddenly drifted to their parents. What an incredible job they must have done raising two such accomplished sons. The pride they must feel seeing both sons in uniform must be overwhelming.

Almost as if he read my thoughts, Arjun softly said, "Our father served in the Army. He took early retirement as Havaldar due to family responsibilities back home. I saw a bit of Army life, but Abhay was very young when Dad retired."

I smiled softly at the two of them, "Your parents must be so proud of both of you," I said genuinely.

"Maybe," Arjun said softly, a quiet warmth flickering across his face. "Even though they never really say it aloud."

There was a pause, a comfortable silence settling between us.

Abhay's stomach rumbled audibly, breaking the moment. He laughed sheepishly. "Sorry, I skipped breakfast."

Arjun laughed, nudging his brother affectionately. "Come on then, let's get something to eat."

Abhay nodded enthusiastically. "As long as it's not mess food, Bhai."

Together, we walked toward Zephyr, it had a café on the ground floor that allowed casual dressing. Arjun's hand gently rested on the small of my back, the subtle pressure sending a thrilling warmth cascading through me, sparking every nerve with delicious awareness.

As we settled into our seats at the café, the warmth of the morning sun filtered through the glass windows. The smell of fresh coffee mixed with the chatter of early diners. We had just placed our orders when I decided to break the ice.

"So, what's the age difference between you two?" I asked, looking between Arjun and Abhay.

Arjun smirked, leaning back in his chair. "Though he looks more mature than me, clearly, he's younger—four years younger, to be precise."

Abhay scoffed, shaking his head. "Yeah, in your dreams." His voice carried the easy humor of someone used to these jabs.

Arjun chuckled. "No, really. He's younger. But somehow, he thinks he's caught up to me."

Abhay leaned forward with a playful glint in his eyes. "Caught up? Bhaiya, I may be four years younger, but my rank is equivalent to yours now."

I frowned slightly, curious. "Wait, what does that mean?"

Abhay turned to me, explaining, "It's just that once you complete your medical specialization and join the armed forces—like in the Army—you directly enter as a Major, which is equivalent to a Lieutenant Commander in the Navy."

I raised an eyebrow, glancing at Arjun, who was now shaking his head, a grin playing on his lips. "And yet," he said, "your training has nothing on mine. I gave my entire childhood to the defense forces."

Abhay laughed. "That's true. I lived the civilian life—went to private schools, did my MBBS through medical school, and then specialized in psychiatry. It was only last year that I decided to join the Indian Army."

He gestured toward Arjun. "But Bhaiya? His entire life has been about defense. He joined Sainik School when he was in sixth grade—maybe 10 or 11 years old at the time. Then NDA after 12th, then INA for Navy training. And of course, special forces. He's been in this world forever."

Their playful banter made me smile. It was effortless—the kind of teasing that only comes with blood ties or a lifetime of shared memories. I didn't have that. My family might look picture-perfect from the outside, but beneath the surface, we're just a collection of quiet wounds held together by Band-Aids and denial. We don't talk about the scars—we pretend they were never there. But what struck me more than the warmth between them was the way Abhay brought out a different side of Arjun. Softer. Lighter. Almost boyish. And I couldn't look away.

Arjun, around me, was always composed—strong, a bit reserved, carrying a weight I could never quite define. But with Abhay, he was lighter. The sharp edges softened just a little. He didn't just speak; he joked, challenged, and played along.

And Abhay—there was something inherently warm about him. Positive. At ease in a way that made you feel comfortable. His energy was infectious, and I found myself genuinely liking him.

Then, just as I was absorbing all of this, Arjun turned to Abhay.

"Aarohi is preparing for a marathon," he said. "So, you've found your partner."

Abhay's face lit up with excitement. "Really, Aarohi?" He leaned in eagerly. "I'm all about marathons! I usually run two a year. But this year, I'm planning to go for the Ironman in Goa. Ironman 70.3, actually—not the full Ironman, but the half-distance version."

I blinked, taken aback. "Oh my God, really? Isn't that huge?"

Abhay grinned. "Actually, I came here today to ask Bhaiyya if he'd do the relay with me." He turned to Arjun. "I was thinking about it, and—"

"Wait," I interrupted, intrigued. "How does a relay work?"

Abhay gestured animatedly. "So, Ironman consists of three parts—swimming, cycling, and running. 1.9 kilometers of swimming, 90 kilometers of cycling, and then a half marathon—21 kilometers of running. In a relay, we split these between three people. I was thinking of doing either biking or running, and if Bhaiyya could take swimming, it'd be perfect since I'm not comfortable, especially when it comes to open water swimming."

I smiled at him. "Oh, that's something we have in common—I'm scared of swimming."

"See?" Abhay grinned. "Aarohi, why don't you join us as well? You can take the running portion since you're already training for a marathon. I'll do the cycling, and Bhaiyya can handle the swimming."

I glanced between the two of them, my excitement rising. "Oh my God, that actually sounds like a great plan!"

Before Arjun could even respond, with a wide grin, Abhay held up his hand, and I met it with a quick high-five.

"Done! It's happening on the 12th of November. I'm signing you both up right now. No backing out."

I laughed. "Wait, what?"

"And I'm paying for it. No refunds," Abhay added with a mischievous grin. "So now, you two have no choice but to come."

I turned to Arjun, who had been silently watching the entire exchange. He exhaled, shaking his head slightly.

Abhay and I had already divided the roles, planned the race, and locked it in—without even waiting for Arjun's agreement.

And just like that, the three of us were doing Ironman 70.3 together in Goa this year!

# Chapter 10: Undressed by His Eyes

## Aarohi

**Evora's Annual Kick-off Event**

Who says you can't make friends at work? Siya and Meher were proof that you could find your people even in the most unexpected places.

I met Meher on my first day at Evora Events. She was supposed to be my mentor, guiding me through the chaos of corporate life. But somewhere between client meetings, late-night brainstorming sessions, and celebratory drinks after stressful events, she became my best friend.

And through Meher, I met Siya—the perfect storm of sharp wit, unmatched confidence, and a heart that cared more than she'd ever admit. The three of us had been inseparable ever since.

Tonight was a big night. The Annual Kick-off Event was more than just a party—it was the night promotions were announced. I had a strong feeling that my name was on the list, but I didn't want to be too confident. I kept my excitement in check, waiting for the moment.

And then, it happened.

*"Senior Project Manager – Aarohi."*

For a brief second, I was frozen. And then I turned, my gaze instantly finding Siya and Meher.

They screamed before I could even react, pulling me into a tight hug.

"You did it!" Meher's voice was muffled against my shoulder.

Siya grinned, gripping my arms. "We knew it, Aarohi. This was *yours*."

I laughed, overwhelmed, happiness blooming in my chest. Two years. Two years of working, building, proving myself. I let the moment sink in. The music thumped around us, the energy in the ballroom electric. My black dress—a last-minute pick—fit like a second skin, the hem teasingly brushing mid-thigh. I felt good. No, I felt powerful.

Wine in hand, I let myself breathe it in—the success, the joy, the unfiltered rush of accomplishment.

And then, my phone buzzed.

I glanced down, my pulse stumbling when I saw the name.

Arjun.

I stepped away from the crowd, raising the phone to my ear.

"Hey," I said, a little breathless.

"Hey," his voice came through, deep and steady. "Celebrating?"

"Yes!" The excitement bubbled out of me. "Guess who's now a Senior Project Manager?"

"That's amazing, Aarohi. Congratulations."

Something about the way he said my name made my cheeks warm.

"Are you drunk?" he asked, amusement laced in his tone.

"Maybe... a little," I admitted, glancing at my empty glass.

"Are Siya and Meher with you?"

"Yes, they're here. Why?"

"Where's the party?"

I hesitated. *Why does he want to know?* More importantly, *why do I want him to know?*

I gave him the address before I could overthink it.

"I'll be there in twenty minutes," he said, his tone leaving no room for argument.

"Wait, Arjun—"

He hung up.

I stared at my phone. My heart was racing.

What just happened?

I was mid-laugh with Siya and Meher when I felt it—the weight of a gaze.

I turned toward the entrance, and there he was.

Arjun.

The world stilled for a moment.

He stood just inside the doorway, his black shirt fitting him too well, accentuating broad shoulders and a lean, powerful frame. Dark trousers, crisp and effortless. A presence that demanded attention, even in a crowded room.

His eyes found mine, and something in his gaze made the air thicker, the space between us smaller.

Siya nudged me. "Is that him?"

I nodded, unable to form words.

Meher took one look at my face and smirked. "You're screwed."

Arjun's movements were unhurried as he walked toward us. His focus stayed on me, but as he reached the group, he turned slightly toward Siya and Meher.

With a straight face, he extended a hand toward Meher first. "Ma'am." A firm shake.

Then to Siya. "Good evening, ma'am." Another polite nod.

Siya and Meher exchanged a look, then simultaneously turned toward me with exaggerated eye rolls, before shaking his hand with an ear-to-ear smile on their faces.

I barely held back a laugh.

Arjun, unfazed, turned his attention fully back to me, his gaze lingering. Without a word, he reached out and tucked a loose strand of hair behind my ear. His fingers barely brushed my skin, but it was enough to send a shiver down my spine.

"You look beautiful," he murmured, his voice low, just for me.

My throat went dry. "Thank you."

He stepped back slightly, his eyes lingering on mine before jerking his head toward the exit.

"Let's go."

The car felt smaller than it should have. Arjun's presence filled every inch of space, his cologne lingering in the air—a mix of something musky and cedar-like, intoxicatingly masculine. My dress had ridden up slightly as I adjusted in my seat, and his gaze flickered down briefly before returning to the road.

His hand brushed my thigh as he shifted gears, the touch lingering just enough to send a spark through me. I didn't move his hand. I didn't want to.

The tension was unbearable. I could feel it crackling between us like static electricity. My heart raced as I stole a glance at him. His jaw was tight, his focus sharp, but I caught the way his grip on the wheel tightened, the way his throat moved when he swallowed.

And then, without warning, he pulled the car to the side of the road.

"What—" I began, but he turned to me, his eyes dark and intense.

"Damn it, Aarohi," he said, his voice low and strained. "I don't know what you're doing to me."

Before I could respond, he leaned in, his hand cupping my cheek as his lips met mine.

The world disappeared.

His kiss was nothing like I'd ever experienced—fierce, hungry, like he'd been holding back for far too long. My hands instinctively found his shoulders, gripping the firm muscle there as his other hand slid around my waist, pulling me closer.

Every nerve in my body was on fire. I was completely consumed by him, by the way his lips moved against mine, by the warmth of his hand on my skin. I didn't even realize I was breathless until he pulled back, his forehead resting against mine.

"You drive me insane," he murmured, his voice thick with emotion.

I couldn't speak. I could only nod, my chest heaving as I tried to catch my breath.

"Are your parents home?" He asked softly.

"No, they are in Canada visiting my brother, they will not be back for another 3-4 months" I whispered.

His lips curved into a faint smile. "Good."

By the time we reached my apartment, the tension had reached a fever pitch. My fingers fumbled with the keys, and when I finally opened the door, he stepped inside, closing it behind him.

"Take me to your room," he said, his voice low and commanding.

I led him in silence, my heart pounding so loudly I was sure he could hear it.

When we reached my room, I suddenly felt self-conscious. My heels and a couple of dresses were strewn across the bed, remnants of my pre-party chaos. But Arjun didn't seem to notice.

He turned to me, his hands resting on my hips as he pulled me closer. His lips found mine again, softer this time but no less intense. I melted into him, my fingers tangling in his hair as he lifted me onto the bed.

With each second, the kiss intensified, became rough. I had been kissed before, but this—this—felt like I was floating, like if I didn't stop, I would be breathless soon.

Lips turned to tongue, the kiss deepened. His hands gripped my waist, his touch possessive, consuming. My body arched instinctively, and I could feel the heat building, threatening to pull me under completely.

And then—suddenly, he stopped.

Took a step back.

Analyzed me.

His eyes roamed over me, taking in every detail.

He reached out, brushed my hair back from my face. I was sure I looked like a mess—dishevelled, flushed, completely undone.

He slightly rubbed his thumb along the bottom of my lip, then leaned in, his breath warm against my skin.

Then, in a voice so low it was almost a growl, he leaned in close—his lips brushing the shell of my ear.

"Good night, baby. The first time I touch you, I want you sober... wide awake... feeling every slow, deliberate thing I do to you. Not when you're drunk."

He pulled back, his eyes dark, smoldering. "You'll remember me. Every inch."

And he left.

Damn.

Who does that?

Who leaves a girl like this—hot, aching, frustrated beyond belief?

I groaned, running my hands through my hair, still reeling from everything that had just happened.

I turned to the mirror, staring at my reflection.

I looked like I had been kissed. Properly kissed. Completely wrecked by him.

I reached up, tracing the same path Arjun's fingers had just touched on my lips. A shiver ran down my spine.

I let out a shaky breath and fell onto my bed, staring up at the ceiling.

There was something uneasy about this.

A strange fear sat in the pit of my stomach, something my body was trying to tell me.

A warning.

A whisper of danger.

I needed to be careful.

I needed to be so damn careful.

# Chapter 11: Bed and Breakfast

## Aarohi

### The Next Morning

*I want to open my eyes.*

*I want to move.*

*But my body won't let me.*

*My arms are heavy. My chest feels like someone's sitting on it. Sweat clings to my skin like a second layer.*

*I can hear voices. Muffled. Familiar.*

*The clinking of utensils. The slam of a cupboard.*

*And then his voice—louder, sharp.*

*"It's too spicy," he says, the words clipped and bitter.*

*My heart rate spikes.*

*I know what's coming.*

*I'm not even in the room, but I know. I'm small again, hiding in the other bedroom, crouched near the slightly open door. The dim hallway light slices the darkness in half. I can see the outline of my mother, standing still, holding a plate. Her shoulders are tense. Braced.*

*He's drunk. Again.*

*His words are slurred, but his anger isn't.*

*The plate hits the floor with a crash.*

*She flinches.*

*And so do I.*

*I clutch the edge of the bed in my dream, nails digging into the sheets. I want to scream. I want to run out there and stop it.*

*But I'm frozen.*

*Because I know what happens next.*

*The sound of feet moving fast. A shout. A slap, maybe. Something worse.*

*My stomach knots so hard it hurts.*

And then—

The doorbell rings.

Shrill. Piercing.

Another ring.

My eyes fly open.

I'm in my bed, drenched in sweat, my breathing shallow.

I blink at the ceiling, trying to slow the hammering in my chest. My hand automatically presses to my heart. It's still racing.

The doorbell again.

Louder this time.

My body finally moves. I push the blanket off, my shirt damp against my back. My legs swing to the floor, and I sit there for a second, catching my breath.

These dreams have been getting more frequent.

Especially since Mom and Dad moved to Canada to stay with my brother.

Maybe it's guilt. Maybe it's distance.

Maybe it's the fear that I'm not there—close enough to protect her.

I drag myself to the door, still in my oversized tee, hair a mess, eyes swollen.

I open it without checking who it is.

And there he is.

Arjun.

As soon as I opened the door, there he was.

Arjun stood with that trademark grin—confident, boyish, annoyingly disarming. A paper bag dangled from his hand, his other buried in the pocket of his pants.

"Good morning, Aarohi—" he began, but then he paused.

Just a second. Maybe two.

His eyes scanned my face, and something shifted in his expression. The smile didn't vanish entirely, but it faded at the edges, replaced by something quieter. Concern.

His voice softened. "Are you okay?"

I froze.

I hadn't said a word. But maybe he'd seen it—the exhaustion in my eyes, the paleness in my face, or the way I gripped the doorframe like it was the only thing holding me up.

Shit.

I blinked, forced a breath in, then shook my head slightly, as if brushing something invisible away.

And just like that, I switched gears.

I straightened up, pulled the corners of my lips into a grin, and stepped aside. "Good morning, Arjun," I said, deliberately bright. "What brings you to my doorstep this early? Couldn't stay away?"

The teasing lilt in my voice wasn't entirely fake. But it was mostly armor.

He watched me for a beat longer, like he was deciding whether to press further. But then, he stepped in, letting the paper bag rest on my desk like he'd done it a thousand times before.

"Brought breakfast," he said. "And maybe…a little company."

"Not a morning person, huh?"

I finally shut the door, wrapping my arms around myself, trying to ground myself, trying to make sense of this surreal morning.

And then it hits me.

Last night.

The kiss.

The way his hands had felt on me. The way I had let myself melt into him.

I tighten my arms around my waist.

He's watching me too closely.

As if he knows what I'm thinking.

"I brought coffee and sandwiches." He says it like it's the most normal thing in the world. Like this is just... *us*.

I glance at the clock. 7:30 AM. Saturday.

I frown. "Why are you dressed for work?"

He shrugs, laying everything out on my bed. "I have a meeting today."

I raise an eyebrow. "Don't you have Saturdays off?"

Arjun just chuckles. "It's not corporate, baby. There's no Saturday or Sunday. If there's work, there's work."

I roll my eyes but sit down, my stomach growling the second I lay eyes on the sandwich.

Spinach and corn.

I hadn't even realized how hungry I was until I took the first bite.

I noticed his eyes lingering around my dressing table, which was covered in perfume bottles, fragrance oils, glass vials and his eyes moved from the bottles to my vision board. I follow his line of sight.

A collage of old magazine cut-outs, printed photos, torn edges from notebooks—all stuck together in a way that made sense only to me. My version of clarity. My version of chaos.

Priyanka Chopra mid-speech on a stage. A black Range Rover glinting in soft light. A cozy flat entrance with a custom nameplate: *Aarohi Sinha*. A couple standing in a gym mirror— his build broad and grounding, her figure almost melting into his, protected. And in the center, a boutique perfume studio.

White walls, dark wood shelves, tiny lights catching on every bottle, my logo scribbled in the corner. Mine.

He doesn't say anything. Just takes it in with that quiet, unreadable look of his.

And suddenly, I feel too naked.

Like he's seen a little too much of me in just one glance.

"Is this your dream, Aarohi?"

I hesitate.

It feels too personal, too exposed, having him see my dreams laid out like this.

I clear my throat. "The black bottles." I point toward the samples on my dresser. "Those are part of it."

His gaze shifts back to them, patient, waiting.

I get up, walking over, my fingers tracing the curve of the small vials. "These are the oils I need to speak to my vendor in Kannauj about. The better the quality of your fragrance oil, the better your base. These form the base notes—what lingers on your skin long after the top notes fade."

I hold up one of the black bottles. "These are blends. You need at least 48 hours to let them stabilize." I turn, meeting his gaze. "Each fragrance has a story, Arjun."

He pushes off the dresser, closing the space between us just slightly. "You do inspire me, Aarohi." He pushes off the dresser, closing the space between us just a little. "And I'm sure you'll build every bit of what you're dreaming."

I laugh, softly. "My dreams have shifted so many times, I've lost count. As a kid, I wanted to be a veterinary doctor—thought maybe I could heal every stray animal in the world. Then I took up biotechnology. And somehow, that path led me to Evora Events... and now, to perfumery."

I glance at him, curiosity tugging at my voice. "But you... you always knew, didn't you? From the time you understood what a dream even was—you were already walking toward it. How does that feel? To know your path so clearly... and just follow it step by step?"

Arjun looks at me, then away—his gaze fixed somewhere far off. "I don't know if I ever *knew*. I just did what I was told. I was in third, maybe fourth grade, when my dad sat me down and said, 'Start preparing for Sainik School entrance.' I didn't even fully understand what that meant. But I listened. I studied. I got selected; I was maybe, 11 years old back then?"

His voice turns distant. "By sixth standard, I was already in a military boarding school. You grow up fast there. There's no hand holding. No softness. It's all routine, rules, resilience. The goal is simple—NDA. That's the mark. That's the path. You don't question it."

He exhales. "And we're taught early—once you're 18, you don't lean on your parents. You stand. You earn. If you're still asking them for help, it's seen as a weakness. Failure. So, you learn to carry your weight early."

I watch him. "And Special Forces?" I ask gently, not sure if I'm overstepping.

A smile tugs at his lips—the first real one in minutes. "That was mine. My choice. I wasn't the top of my class, but I was always athletic. National-level boxer. I liked the idea of testing my limits. Seeing what my body is capable of."

He leans forward a little, eyes shining. "When you're in Special Forces training, you feel like a superhuman. We'd swim eight kilometers a day. Run a hundred. Drop from bridges, crawl through swamps, carry gear that breaks your spine. And you *don't* quit."

He grins, then chuckles. "They torture you until you forget your name—but somehow, you laugh. You look at your coursemates covered in mud, bleeding, freezing—and you laugh. Because that's what pain does. It binds you. In Special Forces, pain *is* the language."

Then, quieter—more reverent, "There's this one drill where they throw you into water, drag you through the sludge until you break. If you sign the voluntary withdrawal form—you're done. Out. No second chances. And when you're that close to giving up... dying feels easier."

My stomach twists. I didn't expect him to open this much.

"And I made it," he says, softer now. "I became a clearance diver. And for the first time, I felt like I was exactly where I was meant to be."

But then the light dims from his eyes. His gaze drops to his leg. "And then... one second."

Just that. One second.

"I wasn't even driving," he says, barely above a whisper. "If I had been, maybe I could accept it. Maybe I'd make peace with it. But I wasn't. And somehow... I'm still the one who lost everything."

His voice breaks slightly. "The certainty I lived with my whole life... is what's killing me now. Because for the first time, I don't know what comes next. When you have a purpose, life becomes easier to navigate. Without it, it's like the blind leading the blind through a directionless existence."

I want to reach for his hand. Say something comforting. But what could possibly ease the ache of being ripped away from the only version of yourself you've ever known?

So, I say nothing. Just sit there, close enough for silence to feel like support. I want to choose my words wisely!

"Arjun," I began, my voice soft but steady, "I know the accident took a lot away from you. Your body doesn't respond the same way it used to. And I get that—it hurts, it's frustrating. But from where I'm sitting... you're still standing."

I looked at him gently, meeting his eyes.

"You still have your legs. Maybe they're held together by rods, maybe they ache more than they used to—but they're there. And the way you describe what happened... Honestly, you could've lost them. You could've been paralyzed. You could've been taken away from everything."

"But you're here, Arjun. You're still walking. You're still serving. You're still an officer in the Indian Navy—a job people dream of, a badge of honor that means something. So, no... you haven't lost everything."

I drew in a breath.

"Have you ever heard the story of the Chinese farmer?"

He shook his head, just slightly.

"There was a farmer," I said, "and one day, his horse ran away. Everyone told him, 'That's terrible luck.' He just shrugged and said, 'Maybe.'"

"The next day, the horse came back—with a herd of wild horses. Everyone said, 'That's amazing!' Again, he just said, 'Maybe.'"

"A few days later, his son was trying to tame one of the wild horses and broke his leg. People said, 'What a tragedy!' The farmer? 'Maybe.'"

"Then, the army came to recruit young men for war. His son was spared because of his injury. 'What great luck!' they said. And the farmer still replied, 'Maybe.'"

I turned to him fully now.

"The point is—we don't always see the bigger picture. What feels like the worst thing right now might turn out to be the exact thing that reroutes us toward something even better."

I held his gaze.

"Maybe the Universe's plans for you are far bigger than you can see from where you're standing."

And then, with a little more strength in my voice, I added:

"And maybe... just maybe... you're not as broken as you think you are."

Before I can process it, he's close, his arms wrapping around me in a hug. A slow, deliberate embrace.

His lips brush against my hair. A soft kiss.

I should be thinking about what this means, but all I can think about is—does my hair even smell okay right now?

I don't get the chance to overthink it.

I blink, still absorbing everything, he stood up, looked at me and said "Thank you" just a plain simple thank you, and then he kissed my knuckles.

But before he disappears completely, he turns back.

"Oh, hey." His voice is casual, but something about it makes my stomach tighten.

"Tomorrow is Navy Trident Night. It's a ball, basically. Aarohi, would you like to be my date?"

I stare at him.

Just stare.

For a second, I don't even register what he's saying.

And then, I exhale.

"Yes." The word slips out before I can second-guess it.

His lips twitch into a knowing smirk. "What time?"

"I'll pick you up at seven."

I nod. "Okay."

Then, before I can think— "Wait, what's the dress code?"

He grins. "I'll be in ceremonial."

I blink. "You're wearing the ceremonial what—"

"But ladies can wear any gown." He cuts in smoothly. "Whatever you wear, of course, you'll be beautiful in it."

And just like that—he turns, walking away.

"See you."

I open my mouth to respond, but he's already gone.

The door clicks shut.

The house is empty now, except for one thing.

His scent. That musky, woody cologne. It lingers—thick, intoxicating, entirely him. I stand there, breathing it in, my arms still wrapped around myself, my heartbeat still unsteady. I don't know why, but every time we part, there's this strange urge to cry. So, I do what I do best—distract myself.

I grab my phone.

My fingers move before I can second-guess it, typing into our group chat.

Me: *Where are you guys?*

*Fashion emergency.*

Because if there's one person who can fix this—who can pull me out of this absolute emotional spiral and help me find something to wear without making me look like a fool—

It's Meher.

She knows everything when it comes to shopping.

And right now, I desperately need a rescue.

# Chapter 12: The Dress Hunt

*I wasn't dressing to impress. I was dressing to destroy.*

## Aarohi

The moment Meher's and Siya's faces pop up on my screen, I already regret this.

Because the second they see me, Siya squints.

And then—her eyes widen.

"Oh my god."

Meher tilts her head. "What?"

Siya grins like a devil.

"You kissed him, didn't you?"

I freeze. "What? No."

She narrows her eyes. "Liar. Look at you. It's written all over your face."

I groan. "How do you always know?"

Siya smirks. "Because you're blushing right now."

I immediately cover my face with my hands. Damn it.

Meher just shakes her head. "Okay, okay, let's focus."

Siya raises an eyebrow. Meher just waits.

"Arjun has invited me to the Navy Trident Ball."

Silence.

And then—

Chaos.

Meher's eyes widen. Siya screams.

"OH MY GOD."

"YOU'RE GOING AS HIS DATE?!"

"THIS IS SO BIG."

I wince. "Guys—focus! I need help!"

Meher exhales dramatically. "Okay, okay. Let's not freak out."

Siya snorts. "Too late."

Meher ignores her. "Meet me at DLF Promenade, Vasant Kunj. Thirty minutes."

I nod. "On my way."

Siya groans. "I hate being left out. I want updates. I want pictures. Hourly updates. DO NOT ignore me."

Meher and I: "We won't."

Siya: "*I mean it.*"

I laugh, ending the call before she can say anything else. By the time I pull into DLF Promenade's parking lot, Meher is already waiting on the ground floor. She is a fashionista. She just knows what works—what color, what style, what fabric. She has a gift. And honestly, I have no idea what she's doing in corporate. She should be a stylist, and I tell her that every chance I get.

"You're late," she says the moment I walk up to her.

I roll my eyes. "By five minutes."

She waves me off. "Okay, we don't have all day. I've already shortlisted the best stores. We'll check three max—I know exactly what will work for you."

I sigh in relief. "Thank god. Because if I picked something from my own closet, I'd look like an idiot."

Meher smirks. "Oh, I know."

Siya's message pops up in our group chat.

Siya: *I WANT PICTURES. DO NOT LEAVE ME OUT.*

Meher rolls her eyes. "Drama queen."

I chuckle. "Let's go."

Meher leads me straight to Zara.

"This is my first pick. If we don't find anything here, we'll move."

I nod, following her in. We go through her options. Some are too basic. Some are too much. Some just feel wrong.

And then—I try on the black gown.

The moment I look at myself in the mirror, I freeze.

It's perfect.

The way it fits every curve, the way it hugs my back just right, the way it's backless but not overly revealing— it's sexy yet elegant.

I run my hands down the fabric, exhaling.

This is it.

But of course—Meher's approval is the law.

I step out of the changing room.

Meher takes one look at me.

And her eyes widen.

Then she grins.

"Babe, you are going to kill him with this."

She doesn't even wait for my response before taking out her phone, snapping a picture, and sending it to Siya.

Seconds later, Siya's reply pops up.

Siya: *OH MY GOD. HE'S GOING TO FORGET HOW TO BREATHE.*

I laugh, shaking my head, my heart beating just a little faster. We added a pair of silver earrings, a simple bracelet, and strappy black heels to complete the look.

Suddenly—this is real.

Tomorrow night, I'll be walking into that ball with Arjun as his Date!

# Chapter 13: Navy Ball

## Aarohi

By the time 7 PM rolled around, I was ready—both physically and emotionally.

My hair fell in soft waves over my shoulders, my makeup was subtle. And the gown—I couldn't stop looking at myself in the mirror. I had spent two hours this afternoon learning everything about Indian Navy ranks. I was familiar with the Army, but not the Navy. That was still a foreign language to me.

So, I sat down, researched every rank—from Sub-Lieutenant to Lieutenant, from Lieutenant Commander to Commander, all the way up to Chief of Naval Staff.

Tonight, I didn't want to mess up.

I glanced at my phone just as a message popped up.

Arjun: *I'm outside.*

7:00 PM sharp.

Typical Arjun. Always punctual.

I inhaled sharply, smoothing down my dress one last time, then stepped outside.

And there he was.

Standing tall by his car. My breath caught in my throat.

The crisp white uniform, impeccable, perfect—the gold stripes on his shoulders gleaming under the lamplight, his badges shining. His black trousers, the cummerbund cinched around his waist, the effortless authority in the way he stood—it was magnetic.

I had seen Arjun in formals before.

But tonight?

Tonight, he was something else entirely in his uniform.

I couldn't look away.

I swallowed hard, my pulse pounding, my body betraying me with every urge to just kiss him right there.

And then he looked at me.

Really looked at me.

His eyes slowly scanned my black gown, darkening slightly. Like he could see through it.

He stepped closer.

His fingers brushed the bare skin of my lower back, trailing lightly, making my stomach tighten in response.

His touch crawled through me, deep into my bones.

My breath hitched.

"You look beautiful." His voice was low and deliberate.

A shiver ran through me. "Thank you," I managed to reply, my cheeks warming.

He walked around and opened the car door for me. Chivalrous. I smiled at him, teasing lightly, "Chivalrous, always?"

"Always," he replied with that faint smirk I'd grown to adore.

The drive to the Navy base was quiet, but thick with unspoken energy.

Arjun's hand never left me—resting on my thigh, his thumb stroking lightly, absentmindedly.

Every stroke sent a ripple of electricity through me. Thanks to the automatic drive, he didn't need to use gears. Which meant—his entire focus was on me. I could feel it. The way his fingers lingered, I barely breathed the entire ride.

When we arrived at the venue, my jaw dropped. The base had been transformed. Trident Night was a spectacle—illuminated domes, couples gliding across the dance floor, the hum of laughter, and the soft clinking of glasses. Everywhere I looked, officers in their ceremonial whites mingled with their elegantly dressed partners. The air was electrified, buzzing with camaraderie and celebration.

Arjun guided me through the crowd, his hand resting lightly on my lower back. Every touch sent waves of awareness through me, and I found myself hyper-aware of every detail—the warmth of his hand, the subtle brush of fabric as we moved. His touch was barely there, but I felt every second of it.

A group of junior officers greeted us. Thanks to my frantic Google research, I could guess their ranks just by looking at their stripes. Some of them greeted me with a polite "Good evening, ma'am."

Ma'am felt so foreign, so formal, I almost laughed. But I composed myself. "Good evening."

A senior officer, Commander Joshi, joined us shortly after, introducing himself with an easy-going smile. "Good evening, ma'am," he said, shaking my hand.

"Good evening, sir," I replied instinctively, only to realize my blunder when he laughed lightly. "Ma'am, you're not supposed to call me 'sir'."

I glanced at Arjun, mortified.

But he just smiled, stepping in smoothly.

"Good evening, sir." He greeted, shifting the attention effortlessly.

The night unfolded beautifully. The DJ played a mix of lively tunes, couples filled the dance floor, and the atmosphere was charged with energy. The food was exquisite, the cocktails flowing freely. The night unfolded like a dream.

As the music shifted to a slower tempo, Arjun turned to me. "Would you like to dance?"

I hesitated for a moment but then placed my hand in his, letting him guide me to the floor.

The first few steps were tentative, but soon, our movements fell into perfect sync. His hand rested on my waist, firm but gentle, while my hand found its place on his shoulder. The warmth of his touch, the subtle pressure of his fingers guiding me—it was intoxicating.

"You're a good dancer," I said, my voice barely audible over the music.

"So are you," he replied, his eyes holding mine.

And then—the music changed.

A Bollywood song.

Suddenly, the floor erupted.

People let go—officers, their partners, everyone moving wildly to the beat.

I laughed, stepping into the chaos, and just like always, my body knew exactly what to do.

I danced.

And then I saw him.

Arjun—watching me.

Smiling.

Trying to match my steps, slightly awkward, slightly adorable.

But his eyes?

Never left me.

The drive back home from the Navy Ball was quiet but charged with an unspoken energy. My head was still spinning from the night—the music, the laughter, Arjun. Even in the silence, the air buzzed with something unfinished.

As we pulled into my driveway, Arjun turned off the engine and stepped out to open my door. Ever the gentleman.

"Thank you," I said softly. I stepped out, smoothing my gown, unsure of what to say.

I looked up at him. "Well, good night."

"Well, goodnight," I said, starting to turn toward my house.

"Aarohi." His voice was low, but it stopped me in my tracks.

I turned back, and before I could react, his hand gently took mine, pulling me toward him.

"I don't think I'm ready to say goodnight yet," he murmured.

The world seemed to pause as he leaned in, his lips brushing against mine in a kiss that was both soft and electrifying. My breath hitched, my hands instinctively pressing against his chest, feeling the warmth of his body through the stiff, pressed fabric of his uniform.

When we finally pulled apart, his gaze was burning.

I wasn't ready to let go.

Neither was he.

My voice barely a whisper—

"Come inside."

# Chapter 14

*If this is a sin, let it be the one I never ask forgiveness for.*

## Aarohi

The moment the door clicked shut behind us, everything shifted.

Arjun leaned against it; eyes locked on mine. Watching me.

I walked over, slow, deliberate. Every step felt louder than it should've. He met me halfway.

His fingers touched my jaw, feather-light. I leaned in before I could talk myself out of it. Our lips met—soft at first. Searching. Questioning. He cupped the back of my neck and angled my head so he could deepen the kiss. His mouth explored mine, as if memorizing it. Hunger. A careful, aching kind of hunger. We kissed like we were trying to crawl inside each other, like it still wouldn't be close enough. Desperate.

Somewhere between kisses and breaths, we stumbled back into my room. I don't even remember how we got there.

His eyes met mine.

"Tell me to stop," he said. His voice was hoarse, his breathing uneven.

I didn't.

My fingers traced every ridge of muscle, and his breath hitched when I kissed just below his collarbone. Broad shoulders. Muscled chest. Bronzed skin. He made me feel like fire and silk all at once. Like he was holding something fragile. His fingers trailed along the length of my spine, slow and deliberate. I felt the tension coiling tighter in my stomach, every nerve aware of how his skin brushed mine, how his lips found that spot just below my jawline that made me forget how to breathe. Pooling around my feet, he took a step back. And stared.

"You're beautiful," he murmured. The air between us felt charged, too heavy. His lips found mine again - deeper. More anchored. He pressed kisses along my shoulder, every place his hands explored, his mouth followed.

I'd never been kissed like this before—it felt like I had walked into the pages of my own dark romance novel.

His hands gripped my waist, possessive, pulling me into him like he needed me closer—closer than skin would allow. He lifted me like I weighed nothing, my legs wrapped around his hips as my back hit the wall. I gasped, his mouth at my neck, his fingers tangled in my hair, tugging just enough to make me shiver. There were no words—only the frantic rhythm of bodies colliding, hearts racing to catch up. His hand slid up my thigh, my nails dug into his back. It was heat and friction and fire and moans. All I know is that when his hands found the zip on my gown, he paused.

And he took a step back.

He didn't say anything at first. Just slowly stepped back. My legs hit the ground.

I waited. Confused. Embarrassed.

I didn't know what to say, so I said nothing.

He looked at me, avoiding eye contact, and then—

"I think you should sleep," he said, voice quiet, strained. "We have to leave early tomorrow. It's a long drive to Kannauj."

My chest tightened.

What?

I blinked. I tried to process what just happened.

My body was still buzzing. My lips were still swollen. My hands were still shaking.

He picked up his phone and turned away.

I didn't ask why.

I couldn't.

Because how do you even ask that? *Why did you stop?*

Was it me? Did I mess this up? Did I push too far?

I stood there, still slightly out of breath, feeling stupid.

So fucking stupid.

He left the room without another word. Closed the door gently behind him.

And I just stood there, in the middle of my room, in a dress that now felt tight in all the wrong ways, my chest aching like something had been ripped out and left unfinished.

I crawled into bed without changing. I hated the silence.

# Chapter 15: Half a man

## Arjun

I want to be hers. Fully. Entirely.

But the truth is—I'm still trying to make peace with the ruins inside me.

How do you promise someone forever when parts of you have already died?

When even your reflection feels like a stranger most days?

I stepped back. Not because I didn't want her.

But because I wanted her too much, too fast.

And if I touched her in that moment, I knew I'd leave behind pieces of the man I used to be—

scars I haven't figured out how to carry yet.

I want her to remember the softness of my hands, not the tremble in them.

To crave the man I'm becoming—not the one still haunted by what he's lost.

Because loving her now would've felt like handing her a storm I haven't learned to hold.

And she deserves a love that doesn't flinch.

I'm only your half-man.

A shadow of who I once swore I'd be.

My dreams wear bandages,

My pride sleeps in a hospital drawer.

How do I love you?

When I can't even carry my own name without shaking?

You deserve a sunrise.

I'm still caught in the rain.

But I'll meet you with trembling hands,

And love you through the pain.

Until then... Will you wait?

# Chapter 16: Drive

## Aarohi

Delhi at 4 AM is a different city.

The roads—usually a chaotic, honking mess—were strangely peaceful. The air carried a crispness, a slight chill that made me pull my jacket closer. As Arjun started driving, I took a slow sip of my coffee, feeling the warmth spread through me.

He glanced at me sideways. "Good?"

I nodded, keeping my gaze on the road ahead. I'd been a little off since last night. I had even thought about cancelling the trip. But visiting Kannauj this weekend was important. I didn't bring it up... even though the question was stuck at the tip of my tongue. I'm biting it down because... I don't know. I feel embarrassed. Or maybe I just don't know how to ask without making it worse.

He took a sip of his own, one hand on the steering wheel, the other wrapped around the cup. I watched him out of the corner of my eye. There was something about early morning drives that made things feel... different. Quieter. More intimate. The sky outside was still dark, the faintest streaks of light beginning to appear on the horizon. He glanced at me again. "Comfortable?"

I smiled, shifting slightly in my seat. "Yeah. You?"

"Perfect."

It felt like we were the only two people in the world right now.

And that feeling?

Soft Bollywood music played in the background, weaving through the quiet hum of the car. Occasionally, Punjabi beats would break through, and Arjun, being Arjun, would turn up the volume for a moment, tapping his fingers against the steering wheel before turning it down again.

Somewhere past Agra, I didn't realise when my eyes slipped shut. A light sleep tugged at me—until I woke up to the soft click of a camera shutter.

I turned, slowly. "Did you just click my picture?"

Arjun didn't even flinch. "Technically... yes."

I raised a brow. "Delete it."

"No."

"Arjun."

He tilted the phone toward me. "Just look."

I glanced at it. The shot was soft, almost cinematic sunlight catching in my hair, my eyes half-closed. Peaceful. I hated to admit it, but it was... a beautiful picture.

I cleared my throat. "Still. Delete."

He shook his head, grinning. "Absolutely not. Frame-worthy."

Then he leaned in slightly, smirk deepening. "What if I make it my wallpaper?"

I narrowed my eyes. "Then I'm taking a picture of you mid-snore and framing it above your bed."

He laughed—loud and shameless. "Noted."

"You're impossible."

"And you're stunning," he said casually, eyes back on the road like he hadn't just dropped a bomb.

I turned back toward the window, trying not to smile. I failed.

His hand—warm, familiar—drifted to my thigh now and then, his thumb tracing slow, lazy circles before returning to the wheel. I wanted to hold it, to close the distance. But after last night, I held back. What if he pulled away again? I couldn't bear the sting of that twice. Why does it feel like there's a secret script we're both reading from—but neither of us is ready to admit we know the ending?

After a stretch of comfortable silence, Arjun glanced sideways at me. "So, what's the plan in Kannauj?"

I leaned back, stretching a little. "Meeting the Nehraji's. They're one of the oldest families in Kannauj, traditionally making fragrance oils for generations. I need to confirm my order with them."

He nodded. "And that's for the raw oils, right?"

I smiled. "Look at you, paying attention."

He smirked.

"So, there are two ways the perfume industry works," I explained. "One is private labelling, where manufacturers create perfumes in bulk, and you just put your brand name on it. It's their formula, their blend—you're just marketing it under your own label. That's how a lot of brands operate."

"So, basically, slapping a name on someone else's work?" he summarized.

I laughed. "In a way, yes. But then there's the second way—you work with your own formulations. That means knowing how to blend, how to extract notes, how to make a scent evolve over time. That's when you're not just a brand owner—you're a perfumer."

"A perfumer," he echoed, like he was testing the word.

"Or 'nez' as the French call it—meaning 'the nose' because a perfumer relies entirely on their ability to distinguish notes."

He hummed, processing it. "And which one are you?"

I grinned. "What do you think?"

He shook his head, a small smile playing on his lips. "nezzzz" in a weird accent. That made me laugh.

I continued, "There's actually a government institute in Kannauj—the Fragrance and Flavour Development Centre. They train perfumers. I did a short program there, and my biotechnology background helped."

Arjun raised a brow. "Of course, you'd go all in."

I reached into my bag, pulling out a small black bottle. "Three of my samples are perfect. Want to try one?"

He shot me a curious glance before extending his hand. I spritzed a little on his wrist.

He brought his hand up, inhaling deeply. A slow exhale followed.

Then he nodded, a smirk curling at the corner of his lips. "This is nice. Actually, really nice."

I couldn't help the excitement that bubbled inside me. "It's called Confidence."

His eyes flickered to mine. "Confidence?"

I nodded. "It's meant to remind you that you're worth it. That you got this. Perfumes bring you back into the present, and this one. This one is for the moments you need to feel unstoppable!"

Arjun was still looking at me, a thoughtful expression on his face. Then, suddenly, he said— "I like how you smell."

I blinked, caught completely off guard. My fingers tightened slightly around the bottle.

As the highway stretched ahead, the warm scent of my perfume lingered faintly in the car. Arjun brought his wrist up to his nose, inhaling the fragrance I had sprayed earlier.

"So how long will this last?" he asked. I glanced at him, smiling. "Depends. Do you know what makes a perfume last longer?"

He gave me a look. "Uh... not really. Just thought some last and some don't?"

I chuckled. "It's about concentration. Perfumes have different categories based on how much actual fragrance oil is in them versus alcohol or water. The stronger the concentration, the longer it lasts." He nodded like he was trying to keep up.

"So, you've got Eau de Cologne—that's the lightest, just about 2-4% fragrance oil. Lasts maybe two hours tops."

"ahhh!"

I laughed. "Good for the gym or layering. Then comes Eau de Toilette, which is 5-15% oil. That one's more common, and lasts about four to six hours."

Arjun nodded slowly, still sniffing his wrist. "And the one you sprayed on me?"

"That's Eau de Parfum—15-20% oil. Stronger, lasts around six to eight hours. It's usually the sweet spot for daily wear."

He raised an eyebrow. "And the strongest?"

I smiled. "Parfum. The real deal. Over 20% oil. Super rich, lasts over 12 hours, sometimes even a full day. But it's expensive and thick."

I continued. "Be careful where you spray—pulse points matter."

His gaze turned amused. "Pulse points?"

I rolled my eyes. "Your wrists, the base of your neck, inside your elbows. Basically, anywhere your skin warms up. The heat helps the fragrance develop."

He turned back to the road, but I could see the smirk on his face. "So, no drowning yourself in deodorant," he said, a laugh tucked beneath his smirk.

I laughed. "Yes! Perfume isn't supposed to announce you five miles away—it's meant to be discovered up close."

We stopped at a roadside restaurant for a quick breakfast. By now, the sun was fully up, the highway busier, but the early morning chill still lingered.

Over a plate of parathas and chai, I casually mentioned, "So... about where we're staying in Kannauj."

Arjun took a sip of his chai. "Yeah?"

I hesitated. "It's a small town. No fancy hotels. Most places are either small guest houses or banquet halls that double as lodges when there aren't weddings."

He nodded. "Sounds fine."

I sighed. "I booked one of those guesthouse rooms for myself... because I wasn't sure you were coming."

Arjun didn't even blink. "And?"

I raised an eyebrow. "And that means you'll have to stay with me."

He leaned back in his chair, his lips curving into a slow, knowing smile.

"Was that even a question?"

I rolled my eyes. "Just clarifying."

He leaned forward, a smirk tugging at his lips, eyes locked with mine. "Ah haan," he said, voice low and teasing. "Like you were ever going to book two rooms."

..................................................................................

**Kannauj**

By the time we pulled into Kannauj, the town was already bustling —narrow streets lined with small, timeworn shops, vendors shouting out their morning sales, the rich scent of attar and spices thick in the air.

Arjun followed Google Maps to our guesthouse, parking just outside.

The place was modest but clean, the kind of spot meant for travellers passing through. I stretched, stepped out of the car, and immediately felt the heat of the sun on my skin.

"We have a meeting with Nehraji at eleven," I said, checking my phone. "It's already past eight, so I'll freshen up. Let's grab a quick bite after that, and then I'll head to the meeting. You can explore Kannauj a bit in the meantime?"

Arjun nodded. "Sure."

# Chapter 16:

*When she enters, the molecules in the air shift!*

## Arjun

Kannauj was unlike any place I'd been before.

The town felt like it had paused in time, holding onto its history. The narrow lanes, the old architecture, the houses with their intricate wooden doors and hand-carved balconies—everything about it felt rooted in something deeper, something older.

I was taking it all in, but my eyes kept drifting back to her.

Aarohi.

She was in her element.

The moment we stepped out of the car, she was on the move. She wore a simple cotton suit—white with a faint blue border. Hair tied up. Silver earrings. She folded her hands and greeted Nehra ji with that calm voice of hers. There were three generations of the Nehra family sitting there—the grandfather, the son, and the younger one who looked barely twenty—the family that had been making fragrance oils for generations.

Today, they were distilling rosewater. Buckets full of fresh petals, steam rising from the old setup, like a scene from a different century.

This is a different side of Aarohi, and I love how fiercely passionate she is about her work—her dream. She knows exactly what she wants and she's not compromising even on the shortest of details.

I found myself watching her through the half-open door, leaning casually against the frame as she spoke to the vendors.

The way she moved between people, shifting effortlessly between politeness and authority, the way her voice held its own weight, how she never wavered when asking for what she wanted. I watched as she carefully examined each bottle design, inspecting the glass quality, the finishing and the dimensions.

Nehra ji was trying to explain something about the cap design. She cut him off—politely, but with directness in her voice. "This click—it's not just about sealing the bottle," she said. "It's about memory. When someone presses it shut, that magnetic sound—it needs to feel like something just got locked in. It needs to *stay* with them."

He didn't get it. Maybe he didn't have to.

The way she described it—how the simple act of opening a perfume bottle could ground someone in the present, how the magnetic click could become an unconscious trigger to reset your mind—I had never thought about it that way.

To me, a cologne was just... cologne.

But to her?

It was an entire world.

She spoke about fragrance the way I spoke about diving.

We hopped from one place to another—she had a long list of people to meet, and not a second to waste. I watched as she gestured to one of the samples, shifting the molecules in her hands, explaining the layers of the scent to the vendor. She was completely unapologetic about her expectations, making it clear exactly what she wanted, exactly how it needed to be.

She was brilliant.

She was a force.

By the time she wrapped up her work, it was already close to 10 PM. The pain in my legs was excruciating—I hadn't walked this much since the accident. My foot had started to swell slightly from being on it all day. The rods in my legs were still adjusting, but I had insisted on walking without the crutch, hoping to force my body to adapt faster. I don't have much time left. I know I'm asking for the impossible, but I want to give it everything I have. I want these rods out of me. I want to go back to the man I used to be.

I ordered dinner to the room, quietly laying everything out on the table while she stepped into the bathroom. But when I turned back, she was already curled up on the bed—half-asleep, completely drained. God, she must've been exhausted. And yet... she looked so peaceful, so heartbreakingly beautiful. I sat beside her, tempted to lean in, kiss her forehead, cup her face—just hold her for a second longer than I should. But just then, her eyes fluttered open and I froze. "Aarohi," I whispered, "dinner's here. Don't sleep on an empty stomach, please." She murmured something about being tired, trying to turn away. But I gently coaxed her up, held the plate in one hand and fed her bite by bite with the other. She let me. Around the eighth bite, she looked at me sleepily and smiled, "Thank you, Arjun." And just like that, she drifted back to sleep. I sat there like an idiot, grinning ear to ear, watching the soft strands of her hair fall over her cheek. I brushed them back, ran my fingers lightly along her temple, and kissed her forehead—barely a touch. I don't know what this is between us. But I do know this: I'm proud of her. And I hope— I really hope—life gives her all the happiness she's chasing. She deserves it. Every bit of it.

## Chapter 17: Scars

## Aarohi

### Kannauj, 5:00 AM

*I wake up choking on my breath. My throat is dry. My skin is damp. My heart is hammering against my ribs, and for a few seconds, I swear I'm still there.*

*I'm home. Or what used to be home.*

*And he is there. And she is there. And I am small again. And I am helpless again. And Dad is towering over Maa, his hands clenched into fists, his voice a sharp, violent thing slicing through the silence. Maa is curled into herself, trying to make herself smaller, like maybe if she shrinks enough, he'll stop seeing her.*

*He doesn't.*

*I scream. I throw myself between them. I grab at his arm, try to push him away, try to stop him, but he doesn't even look at me. I am nothing. A shadow. A whisper.*

*His fist collides with her cheek. The crack of it makes my stomach turn. Blood splatters onto the floor, onto her. She gasps, stumbles, but doesn't cry out. She never does.*

*I do.*

*I scream. I sob. I claw at him, but he is stronger. He is always stronger.*

I wake up gasping.

The nightmare lingers. It clings to my skin, wraps around my bones. I press the heels of my hands into my eyes, trying to shake it off, trying to breathe through it, but the weight of it sits on my chest like a stone.

I turn my head. Arjun is beside me, still asleep. His back is to me, one arm stretched out lazily across the sheets. His breathing is slow, steady. Peaceful.

I swing my legs over the side of the bed. My breath is uneven, too fast. The dreams have become more frequent lately. The distance from Maa only makes them worse. Every time she calls at an odd hour—or worse, when I miss her call—my mind spirals straight to the worst. What if he lost his temper again? What if they fought over something petty again? What if she's alone in that house with him?

I grab my phone. I text my mom:

**All okay, Mom?**

I don't even know if she's awake yet. But I need to send it. I need to know. I always need to know.

Because if I don't—

I press send.

I close my eyes for a second. My heartbeat is still too fast. My skin still feels too tight.

The mattress shifts slightly. I hear the faint rustling of sheets. I don't have to look up to know that Arjun is awake. I feel his gaze on me.

He looks at me and says, "You, okay?"

I nod once. "Yeah."

It's a lie.

He knows it's a lie.

But he doesn't push.

I hear him slip out of bed. I hear the faint sound of water pouring into the kettle. A few minutes later, he sets a cup of coffee beside me.

Arjun picks up his own mug and sits on my side, his hand finds the small of my back, looks into me and says "Whenever you're ready... you can trust me. I might not have a solution—maybe some problems don't have one. But if you ever need someone to just listen, without judgment, without advice... I'm here."

Not sure what it was with his presence, it settles over me like a warm blanket on a snowy night.

"I think this is the worst part of it all.

The guilt.

The guilt I am still struggling with.

The guilt of knowing that the man I hate the most... is also the reason I am who I am today which I am grateful to him for.

My dad.

I don't even know how to explain this properly—he's been a good father in many ways. But as a husband? He was the worst.

He paid for everything. The best schools. The best tuition. A life most people would call privileged. He worked relentlessly and gave us more than we could ever ask for. We had luxuries our friends didn't.

I have everything I have today because of him.

My education. My stability. My choices.

They all exist because he paid for them.

But at what cost?

At the cost of my mother's face being bruised every other night?

At the cost of silent sobs behind a locked bathroom door?

At the cost of constant fear we lived in?

At the cost of my childhood echoing with apologies that meant nothing?

I understand now why Maa never left.

I understand why so many women stay.

Because leaving is only an option when you have somewhere to go.

When you have money. When you have choices. When you have a bank account that's yours.

But if you don't?

If your entire life, you've been told that this is what marriage is?

That this is what normal is?

That your pain is a fair exchange for a roof over your head and food on the table for your kids?

Then where do you go?

Nowhere.

You stay.

You survive.

And that's why I made a promise to myself—

That I would never, *ever* depend on someone the way Maa did.

That I would have my own house. A space that's just mine.

My own money. My own safety.

That no man would ever be able to take anything from me.

Because I would never need him in the first place.

The *only* thing I would ask for—is love.

A love I never once saw in my parents' marriage.

But the worst part?

The part I can't admit out loud?

Some days, I feel grateful that Maa stayed.

Because if she had left...

Where would we be?

And that's what I hate the most—

That during that time part of me was thankful for her staying in that hell. As I had no idea, we had the option to move out!

What kind of daughter feels that way?

Does that still make me a good one?

Today, when I look back, I just wonder—what if she had left? Maybe we would've been in a government school. Maybe we wouldn't have had the best tuition or the brand-name clothes. Maybe I wouldn't have gone to the college I did. Maybe everything would've been smaller. Simpler. But maybe... she would've been happy.

And I hate that I never thought about that before. That I never saw it until much later—until I started earning, until I stood on my own two feet and realised it wasn't as impossible as it once seemed.

What breaks me now isn't just what she went through. It's that I wish someone had told her—really told her—that she could leave. That she didn't have to stay. That she could have rebuilt, maybe slower, maybe harder, but on her own terms.

Maybe that's the privilege I have now—that I get to say I won't tolerate it. That I get to choose differently. Maybe that's what our generation is doing—we're unlearning.

And I hope she knows that. I hope every woman knows that. That they can still leave. That they can still build. That they will survive."

........................................................................................

## Arjun

As I listened to Aarohi, her words cut through the air like shards of glass. Her voice was steady, but I could hear the tremble underneath—a raw honesty she was almost afraid to admit. And when she said she hated herself for feeling grateful that her mother didn't leave.

I wanted to reach out, to hold her hand or touch her shoulder, but she was staring out of the window, lost in her thoughts. The weight of her guilt, her resentment, her gratitude—it all hung in the space between us, unspoken but loud.

I took a breath, searching for the right words, the kind that wouldn't feel like empty consolation. "Aarohi," I said softly, my voice breaking the silence.

She turned her head slightly, her eyes still clouded with emotion. "Hmm?"

"I need you to understand something," I began "The way you feel—it's not wrong. It's not selfish. It's human."

Her brows furrowed, and I saw the doubt flicker in her eyes. But I wasn't going to let her carry this burden alone.

"You know," I said, glancing at her briefly, "we're all products of the situations we're born into. And sometimes, survival isn't about doing what feels morally perfect—it's about making sure you make it to the next day. Your mom... she did what she thought was best. She stayed because she wanted to give you and your brother the stability she couldn't have given you on her own. That wasn't her weakness, Aarohi. That was love. That was strength."

She looked at me, her eyes searching my face as if trying to find the truth in my words.

"And you," I continued, my tone firm, "you don't owe anyone an apology for feeling grateful that she stayed. It doesn't make you a bad person. It makes you someone who understands sacrifice. Someone who's learned from it, who's used it to fuel their own dreams. Look at you, Aarohi. Look at the life you've built for yourself. Your mom would be proud. She is proud."

Her lips parted as if she wanted to say something, but no words came out. Her silence was heavy.

"And as for your dad..." I hesitated, choosing my words carefully. "I know it's hard to reconcile the two sides of him—the father who empowered you and the husband who hurt your mom. But life is complicated like that. People are complicated. He wasn't perfect, but he gave you the tools to break the cycle. To be the independent, fearless woman you are today. And you've done exactly that."

She exhaled shakily, her fingers playing with the hem of her dress. "But I still feel guilty," she admitted, her voice barely above a whisper.

"And that's okay," I said, my voice gentle. "Feel it. Let yourself feel it. But don't carry it like a punishment. You've already turned that guilt into something incredible—a drive to create a life that's your own. That's something to be proud of, Aarohi. Not something to hate yourself for."

"Thank you," she whispered, her voice soft but sincere.

# Chapter 19: Past or Is It Still Present?

## Aarohi

The road back from Kannauj was a stretch of silence and rustling leaves, and the air still carried a faint trail of rose and mitti attar. His collared t-shirt clings to his shoulders, the fabric stretched across muscles that clearly have a weekly subscription to pain. I glance at him for a second too long, then quickly look away, hoping the shadows hide my very obvious blush.

"So," I begin, trying to sound casual.

I had wanted to ask him this question for days now. You know how girls are, right? Our curiosity when it comes to a guy's past is unhinged. We want to know everything. The whole damn archive—past loves, worst breakups, dramatic scenes, everything. And not because we want to judge... but because we want to share ours too. But I hadn't found the right moment. Or maybe I was scared to break the illusion we had built so far—of timing, of what-if, of maybes that didn't require ex-girlfriends in their plotline.

Still, the words had been growing like moss on the walls of my throat. Quiet. Green. Inevitable. I turned slightly, pretending to adjust my seatbelt. Trying really hard not to sound desperate—I asked.

"Arjun," I said, trying to sound breezy and failing miserably. "Can I ask you something a little... personal?"

He didn't even glance away from the road. "Of course," he said. His voice was calm. Open. Which somehow made my stomach tighten more.

"Have you ever been in love?"

He looked at me, one brow raised, clearly not expecting the question. Honestly, neither was I expecting him to answer as seriously as he did.

"Yes," he said quietly.

Oh.

Oh no.

That one word felt like I'd just stepped on a Lego barefoot.

I mean—I knew the answer could be yes. Look at him! He's stupidly handsome, brooding in the sexiest way possible. Of course, someone else would've seen it before I did. But still... Knowing it and hearing it are two very different things.

I cleared my throat and somehow managed to squeak out, "That's... nice."

Nice? Really, Aarohi? That's what you go with?

But the girl in me—the one who lies awake imagining him all on myself: No! That's not nice! My lips pressed together.

"You're just going to drop that and drive on like it's a traffic update?"

"Tell me about her?" I blurted out before I could stop myself.

He glanced at me again, this time slower, then let out a long exhale. "Her name was Ishita."

Even the way he said it—soft, respectful—made my stomach tighten. Ugh, can we just skip this part?

"We met in Mumbai. She was a friend of my coursemate's girlfriend. An air hostess. Or maybe she still is—I don't know. But yes, she was sharp, stunning... carried herself like she knew the world and it knew her. She was beautiful......."

Okay. Pause.

There's something admirable about people who speak kindly of their exes. I respect it. I genuinely do. But—let me just say this—it's nice for Instagram captions, not when you're sitting beside someone who's silently crushing on you and trying not to cry into her oversized t-shirt.

I nodded, trying not to let my face reveal the complete spiral I was having internally.

"And?" I asked, because apparently my masochism has no limits.

"To me, it felt perfect. Life was falling into place—career, family, her. I genuinely thought she was the one, we will be married, have a future. I had no doubts."

He smiled faintly. Nostalgic. A little boyish.

Then it faded.

"We tried to make it work," he said. "But I was posted on a ship soon after. There were weeks without network, days when even if the signal came through, it didn't mean she was available to talk. Misunderstandings crept in. Distance created stories. She felt neglected. I didn't even realize we were drifting until... we already had."

I watched his jaw tighten.

"I think I took her for granted. Or maybe I was just too young to understand what kind of effort love actually takes when you're thousands of miles away. She asked for more than I could give at that moment. I didn't know how to tell her I was already giving everything I had."

"She moved on," he continued. "And then... the accident happened. Three months later, I was in a hospital bed, fractured, broken. Couldn't even sit up. I called her. She didn't answer. I don't blame her. She'd waited long enough."

"She moved on," he said, with a small shrug.

Oof.

My throat felt dry.

"She taught me a lot," he said softly. "And this past year... it stripped me down to zero. I've had to rebuild everything. Ishita was... a part of that old life."

I didn't know what to say. I felt like I should say something wise, something strong. But seriously... Why did she have to be *smart* and *stunning*? Why couldn't she have been like, mildly annoying or obsessed with crazy stuff or something?

Apparently, we're all supposed to be evolved now. Mature. Graceful.

Apparently, when someone talks about their ex, we're supposed to nod respectfully, act unaffected, and maybe even compliment their past for helping them grow into the man they are today

Screw that.

I didn't feel evolved. I felt like someone had poked a tiny hole in my chest and was slowly pouring acid through it. The kind that burns and bubbles and leaves you smiling politely anyway.

I swallowed. My tongue felt dry, like the words had been waiting behind my teeth for far too long. I didn't know where I got the courage to say it—maybe it wasn't courage at all, just impulse disguised as honesty. Even as the words left my mouth, I tasted their bitterness. Sharp. Metallic.

"I mean..." I cleared my throat, already regretting the confrontation. "You didn't talk like someone who's moved on. You talked like someone who... still aches a little."

"What?" he asked, voice steady, but something in his eyes flickered—barely a second long. But I caught it.

There was a beat of silence.

Arjun let out a small laugh—dry, almost inaudible. Not funny-ha-ha, but funny like *you-don't-know-what-you're-talking-about-but-I-won't-correct-you-either*.

He didn't deny it. Not really. Maybe that's why he always pulls away—he still has feelings for her.

I never thought of myself as an insecure person. God knows I've stood in rooms with people who made me feel like a second draft—but I've always held my own.

But in that one moment, I did question a lot of the feelings I was feeling. It made me uncomfortable in ways I couldn't name. The car suddenly felt too small, the silence too loud. I wanted to get out, run, breathe—where though? We were literally in the middle of a highway. Where do I even run from this? From this conversation? Oh god, this is the grave I dug for myself. My stupid curious self. Now I have a problem because he had to be too honest, too blunt like reading out a weather report: "Today's forecast: Catastrophic emotional turbulence with a high-pressure ex-girlfriend system moving in. Visibility: zero. Confidence: shaken. Chances of me screaming into a pillow later tonight? 100%."

# Chapter 19: Ishita

## Aarohi

Saturday mornings at the American Diner always felt like a ritual, and this time it felt different—like home after a long, dramatic vacation. The smell of pancakes, syrup, and buttery toast was still there, but so were Siya and Meher, perched in the red booth like they owned the place. And honestly, we kind of did.

Siya was already halfway through a vanilla milkshake, wearing her oversized sunglasses indoors like the extra queen she is. Meher, in her classic soft-glam mode, was scrolling through her phone, probably halfway through three different reels and a Pinterest board of 'outfits'.

"There she is! Look who decided to grace us with her presence," Siya said, sliding her sunglasses down dramatically as I walked in.

"Please," I laughed, sliding into the booth. "I was literally on time. You two just show up like it's your job."

Meher leaned in with that mom-friend tilt of her head. "Okay, but we need updates. And don't you dare say 'nothing much' or 'I've been busy'. We want gossip."

"Wait," Meher interjected. "What's the catch?"

"Catch?" I frowned.

"There's always a catch, and it's written all over your face" she said, waving her phone like a magic wand. "Ex-girlfriend? Weird habits? A secret life as a spy?"

I bit my lip, glancing down at the menu even though I always order the same thing.

My stomach twisted at the mention of "ex." I didn't want to bring it up, but the words slipped out anyway. "Actually... There's an ex. Ishita."

They froze. Siya's milkshake straw stopped mid-sip.

"Oh, damn."

Meher blinked. "Okay, that escalated quickly."

I nodded. "Her name's Ishita. She was an air hostess or is. Smart, gorgeous, met in Mumbai... long-distance, they drifted apart."

"And how did *he* say all that?" Siya asked, eyes narrowing. "Like casually? Like 'oh yeah, I once dated someone'? Or was it giving 'she-was-the-love-of-my-life-and-I'm-still-secretly-in-love-with-her' energy?"

I groaned. "Siya! Don't make it worse. He wasn't dramatic. He was just... honest."

Meher, ever the therapist, placed her hand gently over mine. "And how do *you* feel about it?"

I exhaled. "Jealous. Which is stupid. I mean, I've never even met her. I don't even know if she's in the picture anymore. But just the way he spoke about her—it was so... honest."

"Honest is worse than dramatic," Siya declared. "At least if he was dramatic, you could brush it off."

Meher nodded thoughtfully. "Okay, so here's what we do. We find her."

"WHAT?" I nearly choked.

Meher, on the other hand, grabbed her phone. "What's her full name?"

"Why?"

"To find her, obviously."

"No, Meher!" I protested. "Please don't."

"Okay but just hypothetically, how do you spell Ishita? Like with an extra 'a' or something?"

"You guys are *ridiculous*," I muttered.

She ignored me, her fingers flying over the screen. "I'm just looking. It's not stalking; it's research. Trust me, I'm an expert."

"Expert in what?" Siya teased. "Creeping people out?"

"I have my methods," Meher shot back with mock seriousness, switching between her two Instagram accounts.

"Let's see. Ishita. Air hostess. Mumbai. Hmm. Dated Navy guy."

"Meher, I'm serious," I said, but she was in full detective mode, her focus unshakable. Siya gave me a shrug and a let-her-do-her-thing look. A few minutes later, Meher gasped. "I think I found her."

"No way," Siya said, leaning across the table.

Siya turned the phone around. There she was—*Ishita*. Laughing in front of a beach at sunset, her hair looking like it was styled by the wind itself. Her profile was open. Of course, it was open. Chic, minimal captions, travel photos, effortlessly pretty.

Meher whistled under her breath. "She's... okay."

"Okay?!" I exclaimed. "She's beautiful."

"She's fine," Siya said nonchalantly, scrolling further. "Nothing special."

I shook my head, the knot in my chest tightening. "No, she's stunning. Look at her. She's so... polished."

"And?" Siya said, tilting her head. "You're gorgeous. Stop comparing." I wanted to believe her, but the photos burned into my mind.

Ishita's effortless beauty, her confidence... Suddenly, I felt small, like a mismatched piece in Arjun's life. I'd never been the kind to doubt myself, but now? Mehar smirked. "You're way better, Aarohi. Trust me, I have an eye for these things."

"She's gorgeous," I said, trying not to sound like I was spiraling. "I mean... look at her. She's like one of those girls who wakes up glowing."

"You wake up glowing too," Meher said immediately.

"Yeah, after five alarms, a coffee, and zero emotional breakdowns," I added.

I tried to smile, but the knot in my chest didn't loosen. Not really.

# Chapter 20:

*Let the Night Say It for Me*

## Aarohi

I wasn't ignoring Arjun.

Not really.

I mean, I was replying to his texts. Just... not as fast as I usually do. Not with emojis or extra exclamation marks. Not with my usual over-excited chaos. I wasn't cold, just... quieter.

And the truth?

I just needed a little space.

Ever since he told me about Ishita, something in me had gone still. I didn't want to compete with someone I'd never met. I didn't want to become the girl who played cool on the surface while unraveling inside. I wasn't insecure, either—not in the obvious, self-sabotaging way. But I also didn't want to become that girl. The one secretly measuring herself against someone she's never even met. The one who acts chill but is secretly rehearsing comebacks in the shower. So instead, I pressed pause. Not on *us*, just on the part of me that wanted to be everywhere with him, all the time, that wanted to orbit around him like a lovesick moon.

He noticed it, of course.

"Everything okay?" "Yeah! Just been a weird week."

"Wanna talk about it?" "I will. Soon."

And he didn't push. Which somehow made me miss him more. Ugh.

But somewhere between working late nights and dodging my own overthinking, I had a mission.

Arjun's birthday was on Saturday.

And I was going *all out*.

He'd mentioned it once, in passing—that birthdays weren't that a big deal for him growing up. Some years, he was out at sea. Some were just low-key dinners with family. He said it like it didn't matter. But that's the thing, isn't it? The people who say it doesn't matter are usually the ones who never got to feel what it *could* be.

So, I decided to go all in.

Because someone should.

And if not me, then who?

I found this dreamy event planner on Instagram—her reels were ridiculous in the best way. Fairy lights. Canopies. Lakeside setups that looked like they were stolen straight from a K-drama. One of her reels showed a canopy on a lake inside an amusement park that shut at 7 PM and transformed into this private hideaway afterward.

The second I saw it, I *knew*.

I booked it.

Heather-toned drapes, fairy lights, low-table dinner, and a playlist I'd been curating for three days straight. A soft mix of his favorites and mine.

The amusement park team would row us out to the canopy just after sunset.

He'd have no clue.

Well... kind of no clue. I *may* have casually texted him:

"Don't make Saturday plans. I'm stealing you."

He replied with a "👀" and a "Should I be worried?"

I wanted to scream YES *but in a good way!* but instead, I just wrote:

"You'll see :)"

I've never been this excited and nervous at once. Planning this surprise felt like knitting my feelings into tiny details—into the food, the colors, the candles, the cake. It wasn't just a birthday plan. It was me saying, *I see you. I care about you. I want this to matter to you.*

So now I wait.

Friday night, curled up on my couch with my phone in hand, I scrolled through the Pinterest board I'd made for the setup. My stomach flipped.

God, please let this be perfect.

Please let him feel it.

Because I think...

I think I'm starting to fall for this man.

And I want the night to say what I haven't yet found the courage to.

# Chapter 21: Everything's Over

## Arjun

I walked into the orthopaedics department, my heart hammering in my chest.

"Jai Hind, Sir."

The doctor barely looked up as he flipped through my file. I knew this file like the back of my hand—every scan, every report, every small note of progress I had fought tooth and nail for. But none of it mattered if today didn't go in my favor.

A call buzzed on my phone—Delhi Headquarters, Navy. I stepped out, gripping the device like it was my last lifeline.

"Lieutenant Commander Arjun, we've received your latest medical assessment."

My breath stilled.

"You know the rules," the officer on the other end continued. His voice was clipped, emotionless. "If within one year your medical category is not upgraded, we are required to reshuffle or remove you from the cadre of Special Forces."

Everything inside me froze.

"Sir," I said, forcing my voice to remain steady. "Is there any other way? An extension? A revaluation?"

Only silence.

"The final decision comes from the medical board," he said eventually. "And you know as well as I do son... only the medical officer can approve a category change."

I didn't waste another second. I bolted toward the Military Hospital corridor, each step feeling heavier than the last.

The sterile white walls of the medical wing had never felt colder. The Marine Medical Specialist for Special Forces, sat across from me, skimming through my reports. My leg bounced restlessly as I waited for him to speak.

He finally looked up; his expression unreadable.

One sentence.

One goddamn sentence and my entire world shattered in front of me.

"Nobody ever gets 100% recovered. Your body will never be the same. There will be limits. You should accept your fate and move on."

A dull ringing filled my ears.

Move on? Move on? How does a man move on from something that has defined his entire existence? How does he accept that the very uniform he lived for, bled for, is now slipping from his grasp?

Everything I had fought for, everything I had built myself to be—gone.

I swallowed the lump in my throat, my hands clenched into fists so tight that my nails bit into my palms. But I refused to let the devastation show.

Not here.

I nodded once, sharp and mechanical. Then I stood up, squared my shoulders, saluted the officer and walked out.

Each step felt like I was walking away from who I was—and stepping into an abyss where I no longer knew who I would become, and I couldn't breathe anymore. My breath turned heavy, sharp, like the air itself didn't want to stay in my lungs. I hated the rods in my legs, hated the way they reminded me of what I'd lost. I headed straight to the pool, stripped down, and started swimming.

The water is silent.

Just the sound of my breath. My body cutting through the surface, my arms moving in steady, ruthless precision.

Lap after lap.

Just motion.

The pool is empty at this hour, the only light coming from the dim lamps lining the sides.

Lap.

Lap.

I don't know how many I've done. I don't know how long it's been.

All I know is that it isn't enough yet.

I push harder. My arms ache, my legs scream, but I don't stop. I don't let myself. I keep going until there is nothing left in me.

Until my body refuses to move.

Until I'm breathless.

Until I have no oxygen left to give.

And when I finally stop, gasping for air at the edge of the pool, I don't feel pain. I don't feel relieved. I just feel empty.

I haul myself out, my muscles quivering, water dripping from my skin. I sit at the edge, looking down at my reflection on the still surface.

And I don't recognize the man staring back at me.

# Chapter 22: Happy Fucking Birthday to Me

## Arjun

The messages kept coming in.

WhatsApp pings. Missed calls.

"Happy Birthday, brother!"

"Hope you're celebrating big!"

I replied to a few. Left most of them unread.

What was I supposed to say? I am not sure I am feeling thankful about anything at this point!

I stared at the ceiling fan above me, the shadow of it circling. It wasn't that I didn't want to celebrate. But I am just not feeling like myself at the point; it's like I am fighting with my own self, my own thoughts.

But then there was *her*.

Aarohi.

She'd messaged me earlier this week— I know she's excited for my birthday and I don't want to disappoint her by not participating in her excitement.

And even though a part of me wanted to cancel everything, pull the blankets over my face and disappear for a while, I knew I wouldn't say no to her.

Because she's never said no to *me*.

Not when I ranted. Not when I was just irritated with my own damn self.

She showed up. Over and over again.

Everything with Aarohi is effortless. Maybe even... too effortless.

She brings calm to my rough sea, an anchor in the chaos I've been drifting through. When she talks about her dreams, her laughter spills into the air like sunshine breaking through storm clouds. She's passion and certainty, warmth and wildness, and with her I feel steady. She's like Hope. Magic.

And yet, something inside me resists.

The last year has been relentless—one battle after another, and I've lost more times than I can count. Everything I wanted, everything I worked for, always seemed just out of reach. So how is it that she, so perfect and radiant, has come into my life so easily? So seamlessly?

It doesn't make sense.

I should be happy. I *am* happy. But there's a weight in my chest, a voice whispering that nothing this good ever lasts. That I'm just waiting for the other shoe to drop. Maybe it's the pessimist part of me, the part hardened by disappointments and near-misses. Or maybe... maybe I just don't know how to accept something this perfect without bracing for it to be ripped away.

Because the truth is—I don't trust happiness anymore. And maybe... maybe it doesn't trust me either.

# Chapter 23: Candles and Cracks

## Aarohi

I waited near the gate, toes tapping on the gravel, heart almost vibrating inside my chest. I had checked everything three times, maybe four—okay, five. The fairy lights were rigged to switch on the moment we stepped in. The lake was still. The sky was blushing that soft Delhi twilight hue.

The planner had outdone herself.

White curtains draped the wooden canopy like it was made for a movie scene. The trail leading to it was lined with candles, glowing softly in glass jars. Flowers everywhere—wild, loose, unarranged. Inside the canopy, a table for two. Low seating. Heather tones. Warm lights. A cake waiting quietly.

I had imagined this moment a hundred times.

The way his eyes would light up.

The way he'd look at me.

And then, I saw him.

He stepped through the gate, hands tucked casually in his pockets, a black shirt perfectly hugging his torso. His hair looked a little messier than usual, and there was a faint weariness behind his eyes. But when his gaze settled on me—really settled—something shifted, and his lips curved into an easy, genuine smile.

He walked toward me, slower than usual. I opened my arms and hugged him before he could say anything. He hugged me back, warm—but something about it felt... different. Lighter. Like he's trying to hold on to something.

Still, I smiled into his shoulder and whispered, "Happy birthday, Arjun."

He stepped back, looking around slowly. First at the entrance. Then the flickering candles. Then the soft glow of the path ahead.

His eyes widened slightly.

And then he looked at me.

"Thank you, Aarohi," he said, voice softer than I'd ever heard it. "This is... beautiful."

He smiled again—tired, grateful, and something else I couldn't place.

"Come," I said, grabbing his hand gently. "I want you to see it."

We walked together, and as soon as our feet touched the beginning of the trail, the first set of lights blinked on.

Then another.

And another.

The path to the lake lit up like magic.

I didn't look at him—I was too afraid I'd start crying if I did. Damn I cry about everything.

When we reached the canopy, the lights inside shimmered to life. The curtains moved with the wind like they were dancing.

The playlist I'd sent the planner started playing—soft guitar, something indie and comforting.

We stepped inside. He looked up. Around. At me.

Everything about him looked quiet.

"I've never had anything like this," he said, barely above a whisper.

I lit the candles on the cake slowly. Hands shaking just a little. I didn't want to rush this. I wanted to live in every second of it.

He stood still, watching the flame flicker, the shadows on my face.

I looked at him and grinned. "Go on. Blow them out. And make a wish" I said, clapping my hands in excitement.

He glanced at me, eyes gentle, then leaned forward.

And just as he did, I began to sing.

"Happy birthday to you... happy birthday to you... happy birthday dear Arjun... happy birthday to you."

He smiled as the last line left my lips.

He looked at the candles, and then at me.

And then blew them out. The flames disappeared.

We both sat down quietly inside. For a second, it was just the two of us and the soft glow of something neither of us knew how to name.

And then, I looked at him.

"Arjun," I said gently. "There's something I've been meaning to say. Something I've been holding onto for a while."

He turned toward me, curious. Still holding onto that softness in his eyes.

I took a breath.

"I..."

And then his phone rang.

The ringtone sounded louder than it should have, slicing through the stillness like a crack in glass.

Arjun looked down at his phone.

I looked too.

Ishita.

No emoji. No last name. No frills. Just... *Ishita*.

And that was enough.

His expression changed—barely. But I saw it.

The way his eyes stilled. The way his chest stopped mid-breath. The way his fingers, which had just moments ago brushed the edge of the cake, now tightened ever so slightly around his phone.

I didn't say anything.

Neither did he.

The phone kept ringing.

He didn't answer.

He didn't decline it either.

He just stared. As if the screen was saying something only, he could hear.

And then, it stopped ringing. The screen went black. But he was still staring.

Still. Silent.

I waited, my smile slowly slipping, my heart thudding in some unfamiliar rhythm.

"Arjun?" I whispered, but he didn't move.

And then—it rang again.

He flinched. Slightly.

And this time... he answered.

He didn't say hello.

Didn't look at me.

Just lifted the phone to his ear and listened.

His face was blank. Too blank. Like every muscle was trying to hold something back.

I couldn't hear her voice. I didn't know what she was saying. But whatever it was, it was enough.

He stood up.

And without a word, without even meeting my eyes...

He walked out.

# Chapter 24

*Sometimes the past doesn't knock—it barges in while the present is still holding out its hand.*

## Arjun

I don't know what was running through my mind. Maybe nothing. Maybe too much. But as soon as I saw the second ring from Ishita, I picked up. I wish I could tell you it was instinct or just curiosity, but the truth is, I don't know why I did it.

"Ishita?" My voice was barely above a whisper, and I saw Aarohi's eyes meet mine, searching, confused, hurt. Her expression burned into my chest like a wound I knew I had just caused.

"Arjun..." her voice came through the phone, cracking, weak, and I heard her sobbing. I froze. Everything else disappeared, even Aarohi's gaze on me.

"What happened?" I asked, my voice sharper than I intended. The sound of Ishita's crying filled the line.

"I need you. Can you... can you come?" she said, her words laced with pain.

My chest tightened. Memories rushed back, uninvited and overwhelming. Ishita laughing. Ishita holding my hand. Ishita... leaving me. I didn't think so. I didn't stop to think about Aarohi, about my birthday celebration, about everything that mattered in this moment.

"Send me your location," I said, barely able to meet Aarohi's eyes before I stood up and left.

Her address was in Malviya Nagar, not far from where I was. My hands were tight around the steering wheel, my mind blank, running on autopilot. I didn't even remember making the decision to come here.

Ishita had called. And just like that, a past I thought I had buried pulled me right back in.

When I reached her place, the door was slightly open, the glow of a dim lamp flickering inside. And there she was.

Ishita.

She was sitting on the edge of her bed, knees drawn to her chest, arms wrapped tightly around herself like she was holding herself together. Her eyes were red, swollen—completely wrecked. I had seen her cry before, but never like this.

For a moment, I just stood there.

She looked up, her face crumbling when she saw me.

"He cheated on me," she whispered, her voice trembling as fresh tears began to fall. "I—I didn't know what to do. I just... I called you."

I inhaled sharply.

Unsure of how to respond. The Ishita I remembered was composed, confident, never vulnerable. This version of her... it felt unfamiliar, like I was looking at a stranger. There was a time when her tears had the power to tear me apart. When I would have done anything—*anything*—to take away her pain.

I nodded slowly, stepping toward her. "It's okay. Take a deep breath," I said, trying to keep my tone calm. "Here, let me get you some water."

I walked into her tiny kitchen, opening cabinets until I found a glass. Every move felt mechanical, detached—like my body was here, but my heart wasn't. Why did I come here? What was I expecting?

When I returned, she was still crying, but softer now. I handed her the glass, and she took it, her hands shaking. She drank in small sips, her breath uneven as she tried to calm herself.

I sat down beside her on the edge of the bed, not too close, keeping a small distance. She placed the glass on the nightstand, her fingers still trembling.

"I'm sorry," she began, her voice barely audible. "I'm so sorry, Arjun. I wanted to come back to you. I've been thinking about you so much these past few months, especially after... after the accident. I wanted to reach out, but I just couldn't."

Her words came out in a rush, and I stayed silent, letting her continue. She wiped at her face with the sleeve of her hoodie, her breaths still uneven.

"I was in a relationship," she said, her voice cracking. "With him. And I... I couldn't leave. You weren't there, Arjun. You weren't there, and I—"

She paused, her eyes searching mine, pleading. "I fell for him. I didn't mean to, but I did. And then I couldn't come back to you. I couldn't face you. It would've been wrong. But I hated myself for it. And when I heard about your accident... I felt so helpless. I wanted to come, but I couldn't. It wouldn't have been fair to anyone."

Her words lingered in the air, each one hitting me like a wave. I leaned forward, resting my elbows on my knees, staring at the floor.

And then, suddenly, she hugged me.

Her arms wrapped tightly around my torso, pressing herself against me. I felt the dampness of her tears against my skin, her breath coming in uneven gasps.

And that's when it hit me—my hands wouldn't move.

I stood frozen.

Ishita was hugging me, but my body refused to hold her back.

I tried—I really did. But my hands just wouldn't lift.

Everything felt wrong.

I wasn't sure when it had happened, but my body had become a stranger to this woman.

She trembled in my arms, clinging to me, as if I was the only solid thing in her world. But all I felt was a suffocating detachment.

I needed to leave.

I needed to get out of here.

And just when I thought it couldn't get worse, she pulled back slightly. Her face was too close—her lips inches away from mine.

No.

She was looking at me with an expression I had seen before.

She was about to kiss me.

I took a sharp step back, breathing heavily.

"Ishita," I said, my voice coming out sharper than I intended.

She blinked, startled by my reaction.

"No," I said, firmer now.

Her brows furrowed. "Arjun...?"

I exhaled, running a hand through my hair. "I'm in a relationship."

She froze, like I had just spoken a foreign language.

"What?" she whispered.

I took another step back, putting more distance between us. "I'm with someone. Her name is Aarohi."

Her lips parted slightly, as if trying to process my words.

"And I *love* her."

She flinched like I had slapped her. Ishita swallowed hard, her eyes glistening. "You love her?"

"Yes."

There was a pause, the weight of those words settling into the space between us. We don't always know who we love—until we're standing in front of someone we no longer do.

"Ishita..." I began, my voice quieter than I expected. "I used to think that what we had was love. I spent so much time convincing myself of that. I made it the center of my universe. But now... sitting here, listening to you..."

I paused, looking up at her. She was staring at me, confused and hurt.

"It wasn't love," I continued, my voice firmer now. "It was something else. Something I thought I needed because I couldn't have it. And when you're chasing something, you can't have, it becomes larger than life. It becomes this... obsession. But it's not real. All this time I thought I'd missed you, but I just missed the idea of you."

She blinked, her lips parting in disbelief. "What are you saying, Arjun? That what we had wasn't real?"

I shook my head. "No, I'm not saying that. It was real, Ishita. At least for a time. But it's not what I thought it was. And I think you know that too."

Her shoulders sagged, and she looked away, her tears slowing. "I don't know, Arjun. I still regret not being there for you. I'm so sorry for that."

I smiled faintly, a bittersweet ache filling my chest. "I don't blame you, Ishita. I don't. You did what you thought was right, and so did I. But..." I hesitated, the words catching in my throat. "I've moved on. I didn't realize it until now, but I have.

Her eyes widened as she stared at me.

My voice stayed steady. "Her name is Aarohi. And she's... everything. She's kind, and strong, and... she makes me want to be better. She's the one, the one who makes me feel like I'm alive again. And being here, with you now... it's only made me realize how much I care about her."

Ishita's face crumpled, and she nodded slowly. There was a long silence between us, heavy but peaceful. I stood up, smoothing out my shirt.

"Take care of yourself, Ishita," I said, offering her a small smile.

Ishita wiped her tears. "Happy birthday, Arjun," she said softly, almost as an afterthought.

I chuckled, shaking my head. "Thanks," I murmured, heading for the door.

I didn't look back.

As I walked out into the cool night air, I felt lighter, as if a weight I'd been carrying for a year had finally lifted. But then reality hit me.

Aarohi.

I'd left her. I'd left her on my birthday, the night she'd planned something beautiful for me, because I couldn't let go of my past.

"Fuck," I muttered under my breath, running a hand through my hair. I had to make it right. Somehow, I had to make it right.

# Chapter 25: Half-Loved

*"The hardest part isn't losing him—it's realizing he was never really mine to lose."*

## Aarohi

I sat there long after he left.

The candles had melted halfway, their flames flickering like they, too, were uncertain of what remained. The lake was still, but the night was creeping in fast blue turning to black, shadows stretching longer, the fairy lights dimming around me.

I didn't cry at first.

I just sat there. Staring at the space where he had been.

I picked up my phone. Opened our chat. Typed:

Where are you?

I didn't call. I couldn't. My fingers wouldn't move.

So, I sent the text and waited. One minute. Five. Ten. Thirty.

No reply.

The quiet became unbearable.

And then it hit me. The ache, the embarrassment, the helplessness.

I had planned everything—every light, every flower, every second.

And he left me.

Just... left.

I wrapped my arms around myself as the tears came—sharp, sudden, suffocating. My chest heaved as I finally allowed myself to break.

I didn't even realize I'd called Siya until I heard her voice.

"Hello?"

I couldn't speak at first. My breath hitched. Then came the whisper, almost childlike, "Siya... can you please come get me?"

She didn't ask questions. Just said, "I'm on my way."

Forty minutes later, her car pulled up near the park's back gate. I climbed in silently. The second the door shut behind me, I fell apart again. I cried the whole drive home. Just open, loud, messy grief.

"What happened?" Siya asked, her voice tight with concern. "Aarohi... what happened?"

I could barely get the words out. "He just... left me there."

She looked at me, shocked. "What do you mean he left? What are you saying?"

"I mean," I said, voice shaking, "he got a call... and he walked out. He just stood up and walked away."

"That doesn't make any sense," Siya said, eyes flashing in the rear-view mirror.

I stared out of the window, barely blinking. "Nothing makes sense anymore."

We reached home. I didn't say anything. I just went straight to my room, crawled into bed, and pulled the blanket over me like it could protect me from this kind of hurt.

A few minutes later, Siya walked in holding a mug of coffee. She placed it on the side table and sat at the edge of the bed.

"Aarohi," she said gently. "At least talk to me. What happened?"

I pulled the blanket down slightly, eyes swollen, voice hoarse.

"Ishita called."

Siya's brows pulled together instantly. "What?"

"I saw her name on his phone. And then he left."

There was a beat of stunned silence. Then she muttered, "That fucking bastard."

I didn't say anything. I didn't defend him. I didn't have the strength.

"Aarohi, just talk to him. Maybe it's not what you think."

My voice was soft but sharp, like a shard of glass cutting through the air. "It doesn't matter what I think, Siya. He chose her. On his birthday—on the day I poured every ounce of love into making him feel seen. I wanted to tell him I love him, Siya. Love him with everything I know how to love. But he left me. For her."

"Aarohi..." she started, but I cut her off.

"Do you know the difference, Siya? When a woman cheats, the first question a man asks is, 'Did you sleep with him?'

Because for them, it's about possession. It's the body that betrays. But for a woman..."

My voice cracked. I pressed a hand to my chest, like I could hold the ache in place.

"For us, the first question is always, 'Do you love her?' Because that's what we break over. The heart. The connection. The emotional intimacy. The space in his soul he gave to someone else. And I saw it, Siya. I saw how one call from her shattered him. His face went white. His hands trembled. I know that look. I know what it means. He still loves her. She still lives somewhere inside him."

I sank onto the edge of my bed, staring blankly at the lit screen. "Do you know what hurts the most, Siya? It's knowing that maybe when I looked at him with all the love in the world, he was already thinking of her."

Siya stayed silent on the other end.

I laughed bitterly, though it sounded more like a sob. "Do you know how it feels, Siya, to love someone who is half yours and half someone else's? It's like holding onto a mirage—beautiful, fleeting, but never truly yours. And yet, you can't stop. Because even the half they give you feels like the world."

My throat tightened as tears blurred my vision. "Ishita doesn't need to win him, Siya. She's already won. She's always had his heart. I was just a temporary refuge. A distraction. A consolation prize."

"Aarohi, stop it, enough!" Siya finally spoke, her voice firm but gentle. "You're not a consolation prize. Arjun loves you. You know he does."

I shook my head, though she couldn't see me. "Love isn't leaving someone on their birthday to go to someone else. Love isn't silence when you need answers. Love isn't..." My voice faltered as the tears spilled over. "Love isn't this."

Siya sighed on the other end, her silence both comforting and crushing.

I stood and walked toward my dresser, where the picture of Arjun and I from the Trident Night still stood. His smile, so genuine. My eyes, so hopeful. How foolish I had been to think I could compete with the ghost of a love he still carried.

"I can't be second, Siya," I whispered. "I can't live knowing I'm just a placeholder for the person he truly wants. It's killing me."

The line went quiet, and I knew she didn't have the words to console me. I sat on the floor and stared at the ceiling, my mind racing with questions I'd never have the courage to ask Arjun.

*Did you love her more? Did she make you happier? Was I ever enough?*

But the one question that echoed the loudest was the one I feared the most:

*Did I ever really have your heart?*

# Chapter 26: Not Today

## Aarohi

The morning light sliced through the misty Delhi air, sharp and unrelenting. My eyes still burned from last night's tears, but I didn't have the luxury to fall apart—not today. I splashed cold water on my face, tied my hair into a neat ponytail, and slipped into my crispest formal suit. Today mattered. The ache in my chest would have to wait.

This was the day.

My first investor meeting for Nocturnal Essence.

I had dreamed of it, prepared for it, practiced my pitch in front of the mirror until the words felt like they were stitched into my soul. I hadn't told anyone—because I didn't want to jinx it.

*I can't mess this up.* Not today.

As I walked out to my car, my breath hitched when I saw him—Arjun. He was standing there in his perfectly ironed white Navy uniform. The sun glinted off the golden insignias on his shoulders. He looked like everything I once believed in, everything I had wanted, and everything I didn't know how to handle anymore.

"Aarohi," he said, his voice low but pleading. "Can we please talk?"

I opened my car door, pretending not to hear him. But he moved closer, the proximity making my chest tighten.

"Please, Aarohi. At least give me a chance to explain," he continued, his voice cracking just slightly.

I turned to face him, my face betraying no emotion, though I felt like screaming. "Explain what, Arjun? What do you want to explain?"

He flinched as though my words had physically hit him. "I... I made a mistake. I know there's no excuse—there's nothing I can say to undo it. But I... I'm sorry."

A bitter laugh escaped my lips. I didn't want it to, but it did. "Sorry?" I repeated, shaking my head. "Do you even understand, Arjun? Just one call. One call from your past, and you ran. You left me sitting there, humiliated, wondering what I did wrong, why I wasn't enough. You didn't even have the decency to explain. Do you know how that felt?"

"Ishita..." he began, but I cut him off with a raised hand.

"Don't. Don't say her name. Don't make this about her. This is about you. About how you made a choice, Arjun—a choice to leave, to abandon me without a single word." My voice trembled, and I bit my lip hard to stop the tears that threatened to spill again.

He took a step closer. "Aarohi, I swear, I didn't mean to hurt you. I was... I don't know what I was thinking. I just—"

"You didn't think at all!" I interrupted, my voice rising. "If you had, you would've known that I would've understood. Whatever it was—your confusion, your emotions, your unfinished business—you could've talked to me. But instead, you chose to shut me out. You made me feel like I didn't matter." My eyes burned with fury. I had never felt this kind of anger before. My voice was shaking. "You said you loved each other, right? Well, let me tell you something—when you love someone, you *commit*. You don't walk away. Not because of distance. Not because of pain. Not because life throws some messed-up shit your way.

You *figure it out*.

The moment it gets hard, you don't go searching for the next placeholder.

You *fucking fight*—to be with each other, not from each other."

Arjun looked down, his jaw tightening. He had no words, and the silence between us was deafening.

I couldn't do this anymore. My heart was barely holding itself together, and I couldn't let it shatter again. I turned, got into my car, and started the engine. He stood there as I reversed out of the driveway.

I couldn't breathe.

My body was shaking. Hands were trembling. Eyes got blurry. I blinked hard, but the tears didn't stop. I wiped them away, again and again, but they kept coming. I couldn't stop crying. I didn't even know if I was breathing right. Everything felt tight. My throat. My chest. My shoulders.

# Chapter 27:

*Sometimes we don't ruin people with our hands—we ruin them with our absence, our delay, our silence.*

## Arjun

Looking at Aarohi broke me. It broke me in ways I didn't think I could still be broken. Her swollen eyes, her trembling hands, the faint redness on her cheeks, I had done that to her. I had always seen her smiling. Aarohi always found a way to make me laugh, to make me feel good, to make me feel like I was worth something, even when I didn't believe it myself. And now, I was the reason that her light was gone.

She didn't need to say anything. Her silence screamed louder than any words ever could. And in her silence, I saw my reflection—a man too lost in his past to accept the love standing right in front of him.

I knew she loved me. I had known it all along. The way she looked at me, the way she stayed patient, the way she cared for me without asking for anything in return. And I knew, deep down, that she wanted me to say it too. She wanted to hear the words. But I couldn't. I never could.

Because until now, something held me back. A shadow of a memory, a lingering piece of Ishita that refused to leave. And when Ishita called, when I finally saw her again, everything clicked. Everything I thought I had been holding onto wasn't real. It was a ghost I had been chasing, a feeling I had inflated in my mind, making it so much bigger than it ever was.

But it's too late now, isn't it?

I had broken her. Aarohi, the woman who had stepped into my life to heal me, to help me, to remind me of who I could be—I had shattered her into pieces. And seeing her this way broke me too.

I shouldn't have let her in. I shouldn't have let her love me when I was too broken to love her back. I shouldn't have allowed her to believe in me, to think that I was capable of being the man she deserved.

But I did.

And I have no words to explain myself. No words in this world can justify what I've done to her. What could I possibly say? That Ishita's one call broke me? That a single voice from my past unraveled me, made me run?

How could I tell her that I love her, when I realized it only after seeing Ishita again? How do I look into her eyes and explain that the clarity I needed came too late?

I've ruined it. I've ruined the one thing—the one person—who could have saved me.

And now I have to live with that.

# Chapter 28: It's Time

## Aarohi

The conference room was all sharp lines and clean edges—glass walls, matte black chairs, minimalist everything. I sat at one end of the table, palms pressed flat, laptop open, pitch deck glowing.

**Nocturnal Essence – A Scent Beyond Memory**

**Founder: Aarohi Sinha**

I'd rehearsed this moment more times than I could count. My pitch. My pacing. The numbers. The customer feedback loops. The market cap. The why.

Every answer was memorized.

And across from me sat Devika Rao, co-founder of one of the top venture capital firms in the country. Mid-forties. No-nonsense bun. Black power suit. The kind of woman whose silence makes a room stand straighter.

She listened. Hands folded. Face unreadable.

I clicked to the first slide and began.

"Nocturnal Essence is a sensorial perfume brand rooted in memory, emotion, and India's olfactory heritage. Our unique blends are built on three core principles: nostalgia, individuality, and quality. We've grown 23% quarter-on-quarter for the last two quarters..."

I moved through the slides, voice steady.

Customer retention. Repeat purchase windows. ROI. Cost per acquisition.

She didn't interrupt. Just watched me.

Slide by slide, I laid it all out—my heart, my strategy, my soul. This wasn't just perfume. This was *me*, bottled.

Finally, halfway through my sixth slide, she raised her hand gently.

"Can I ask you something, Aarohi?"

I paused. "Of course."

"What do you currently do?"

The question was soft. Casual even. But I felt my body stiffen.

"I'm currently working full-time at Evora Events as a senior project manager," I said, my tone polite, controlled. "Nocturnal Essence was built alongside that. Nights, weekends. I've hired freelancers for design, fulfillment, and social media. And I handle the strategy, customer communication, and brand development myself."

Devika nodded slowly.

Then she tilted her head. Her voice didn't change, but something in her eyes did.

"You're asking me to invest real capital. To believe in your dream with you. But tell me, Aarohi... how do I trust a brand whose own founder hasn't trusted it fully yet?"

My breath caught.

"Ma'am, I—"

I paused. The words stuck.

"You have a cushion," she continued gently. "Your job. Your salary. If this doesn't work, you'll be okay. You have a net. But me? I'm jumping in with both feet. No net. So how do I follow you, when you haven't jumped yet?"

It wasn't harsh.

That's what made it worse.

It was honest. Quiet. True.

And it landed somewhere deep in my gut—because I'd asked myself the same thing in the mirror a dozen times. I'd just never said it out loud.

I couldn't answer. Not really.

Devika looked at me one last time, her expression—just... settled.

"When you're ready to give it everything," she said, sliding a card across the table, "call my assistant. I'd like to have this conversation again."

She stood up. Adjusted her blazer. Extended a hand.

I took it. My grip firm even though my pulse was everywhere.

"Thank you for your time," I said. "You'll hear from me again."

"I hope so," she replied, and walked out.

The door shut with a softness that felt like a full stop.

I sat down again.

Just me.

The hum of the AC.

And the final slide on the screen.

**Founder – Aarohi Sinha**

I stared at it.

My name.

My dream.

My fear.

And then I whispered, almost like a promise to myself—

"It's time."

# Chapter 29: I fucked up!

## Arjun

Abhay is standing in front of me in my room.

I'm sitting on the edge of my bed, feeling lost. Feeling like shit. Feeling absolutely miserable, with an ache in my chest so deep it feels like it's cutting straight through me.

I know I need to go and convince Aarohi.

But what the fuck do I even tell her—when I'm not in my own senses right now?

Abhay doesn't say anything. He just looks at me, his face unreadable. He's analyzing, processing—doing what he does best. And then, without a word, he moves.

He pulls out the whiskey from the cabinet, pours two glasses, and hands me one.

I take it in one long sip, down in an instant.

He pours another.

I hold the glass in my hand this time, the burn of the alcohol nowhere near as bad as the burn inside my chest.

I look at him. My voice is hoarse when I say it.

"I fucked up."

He still doesn't speak. Just watches me, waiting. I think that's where his psychiatrist training kicks in. Maybe, at this moment, he's looking at me like a patient.

Like someone too far gone.

But he waits. Because he knows I'll say more.

And I do.

"I fucked up." I exhale, shaking my head. "I got one text from Ishita, and I ran back to her. I went back running toward Ishita."

But then I pause, my throat tight.

"But you know what, Abhay? It wasn't even about Ishita."

I was running toward a life that doesn't fucking exist anymore.

A life where everything was perfect.

Where my job wasn't this meaningless bullshit. Where my relationship was stable. Where I didn't wake up every day with a hollow chest and a useless fucking leg.

I let out a rough, bitter laugh.

"You know what it takes to become a clearance diver?"

Abhay stays quiet.

"You bleed. You starve. You're tortured. You don't sleep. You push your body to the edge of death, and even when you're about to collapse, you keep going. Because you would rather die in training than give up."

I stare at my glass, my knuckles white from holding it too tight.

" Jumping off bridges into black water where you can't see shit. Crawling through the mud. Freezing nights. Days when you haven't eaten in thirty-six hours, but you still move. Because your body isn't yours anymore. It belongs to a purpose."

"And then one day—one fucking accident—" my voice catches, and I force myself to swallow it back.

"One accident. And it was over."

I look at Abhay.

"I wasn't even driving. I was just sitting in the fucking vehicle. And the guy driving? He walked away without a scratch. But me? My leg was gone. My career was gone. And just like that—" I snap my fingers, "—everything I had killed myself for was taken away from me."

I laugh again, but it's sharp, bitter.

"And now what? Now, I'm good enough for paperwork. Good enough for just office duties like a liability to force! That's what I'm worth now."

I drag my hands down my face.

"That text from Ishita? It wasn't about her. It was never about her. It was about a life that called me back, a life where I still had everything. I just—" I take a shuddering breath, "—I just wanted to feel like myself again. Even if it was a lie."

And now my hands are shaking. My throat tightens. My chest hurts.

I can feel my eyes burning, my vision blurring, and I don't even try to stop it.

Because this is it.

I have nothing left.

I'm nothing.

I let out a shaky breath, my voice breaking.

"I will never be good enough again, Abhay."

And in this moment, how the fuck do I explain that to Aarohi?

How do I look her in the eyes—this girl who has done everything right by me, who has tried to make me feel alive again, who has given me a reason to want more—

And tell her that nothing makes sense anymore?

That she can't fix this.

That no one can.

That I feel like a fucking failure.

My chest is still heaving, my knuckles white around my glass. My entire body is screaming in exhaustion and grief.

This is about loss.

The loss of identity.

The loss of purpose.

The loss of the man I thought I was meant to be.

Finally, Abhay speaks.

"You're grieving."

It's not a question. It's not a suggestion.

It's a fact.

My head snaps up, my bloodshot eyes narrowing. "What?"

Abhay leans forward, his elbows resting on his knees, voice steady.

"You're grieving the death of yourself. The version of you that you built with your own blood, sweat, and pain. The version of you that made sense."

I stare at him, breathing hard, my jaw tight.

He doesn't look away.

"People think grief is just for the dead. But that's not true. You can grieve a person, yes—but you can also grieve a life, a dream, a future that you built for yourself, only to have it taken away."

My jaw clenches, but I don't interrupt.

"You pushed your body beyond human limits, Arjun. You trained until your cells forgot how to do anything except obey. You built a version of yourself that was invincible. And then—" Abhay's voice softens, "then, life reminded you that you weren't."

I exhale harshly, shaking my head. "So what? What the fuck am I supposed to do with that?"

Abhay tilts his head, studying me.

"The same thing anyone does when they lose something they love. You mourn it. You allow yourself to grieve it. But most importantly—" he pauses, making sure I'm really listening, "you learn that you are more than it."

I look away, my throat bobbing. "That was all I was."

Abhay shakes his head. "No, that was all you believed you were."

Silence.

I don't move, but my mind is racing.

And Abhay knows it.

So, he keeps going.

"You keep saying you'll never be good enough again. But for what, Arjun? For the life you used to have? The one that doesn't exist anymore? Of course, you'll never be good enough for that. Because it's gone."

He leans back, voice unwavering.

"But you're not."

I exhale sharply, like the words hit somewhere too deep to acknowledge yet.

Abhay watches me carefully.

Then, in a quieter voice, "You were trained to push through pain, to survive no matter what. So why is this any different?"

I let out a bitter laugh. "Because this isn't a battlefield or training ground, Abhay."

His gaze doesn't waver.

"Isn't it?"

I freeze.

Abhay leans forward again.

"You've survived hell before. You trained your body to withstand the unthinkable. You pushed past pain, exhaustion, fear, and you came out stronger."

He lets the words settle before delivering the final blow.

"So why are you so sure you can't survive this?"

My breath stutters, my fingers tightening around the glass.

Abhay doesn't push further, and leaves. I fall into bed, my body exhausted, but my mind refuses to shut down.

I reach for my phone before I can stop myself.

I stare at the last message from Aarohi.

"Where are you?"

Just a question mark.

She hasn't reached out since.

I start typing.

Aarohi, I need to speak with you. I'm so sorry. I need to explain to you.

My thumb hovers over the send button.

I can't do it.

Not yet.

I let out a sharp breath, pushing my phone away, leaving the message in drafts.

The temple bells are ringing in the distance.

I don't consciously walk toward them. My legs just carry me there.

The temple isn't crowded at this hour. A few devotees are scattered, some lighting diyas, some whispering prayers, some just sitting in silence.

I step inside.

I don't pray to any one specific god.

I never have.

But I sit down, staring at the idol in front of me, my arms resting on my knees, my breath slow.

I close my eyes.

And without a sound, a single tear rolls down my cheek.

I don't wipe it away. But then came the second. And the third. I looked straight at the idol and tilted my head toward the sky, willing the tears to stay inside my eyes. But they refused to listen. I shut my eyes tight, trying to send them back.

I just sit there. I don't know how much time passes. Maybe 45 minutes. Maybe 50. Maybe more. Long enough for my legs to go numb. Long enough to feel everything and nothing at once.

I just breathe.

I just be.

And when I finally open my eyes, I look at the idol one last time before stepping outside.

I see him the moment I leave the temple.

A small child, barefoot, standing near the steps, looking up at passers-by with an empty steel bowl in his hands.

He glances at me hesitantly, then looks away.

I crouch down. "Are you hungry?"

He nods.

I stand. "Come."

I take him to the closest food stall. The air smells of spices and fried dough, the sizzle of oil loud against the quiet street. He went for a plate of chole bhature.

The vendor serves it fresh, hot. The boy's eyes light up, his fingers digging in immediately, stuffing a bite into his mouth.

I just watch him eat.

And suddenly I heard Aarohi's voice in my subconscious, soft but certain.

*"When life feels unfair, just do an act of kindness. You'll understand the world better."*

I exhale.

And for the first time in what feels like forever, I slightly felt something settling.

Something a little less heavy.

# Chapter 30: The First Goodbye

## Aarohi

I stared at my laptop screen, the resignation email sitting in my drafts folder, taunting me. Every word had been carefully chosen, each sentence rewritten at least twice. My cursor hovered over the "Send" button, but I couldn't press it.

Evora Events wasn't just a job to me—it was my first step into adulthood, my first taste of independence. This company had given me so much, and leaving it felt like a breakup with a part of myself. I couldn't just send an email and walk away. I owed Tanya, my manager and mentor, a face-to-face conversation.

I remembered my first day here like it was yesterday. The nerves, the excitement, and most of all, the determination to make an impression. The interview process had been intense. Hundreds of students, all with similar grades, similar internships, similar resumes—it was a sea of sameness.

But I wanted to stand out. So, I did something different. I created a one-page deck in Canva—a clean, bold presentation outlining how I could contribute to Evora Events. I listed my skills, my ideas, and most importantly, how I could bring value to their team. I printed it, attached it to my resume, and walked into that interview with quiet confidence.

When the panel started asking the standard questions, I slid the page across the table. I'll never forget the way Tanya, who was one of the interviewers, paused and smiled as she looked at it. From that moment, the conversation shifted. It wasn't about generic answers anymore—it was about me, my ideas, and my potential. And at the end of it, Tanya chose me for her team.

She had been my guide ever since, shaping me from a clueless fresher into someone confident, capable, and ready to take on the world. Walking into her cabin now felt surreal, like coming full circle.

Tanya looked up from her laptop, her warm smile instantly calming my nerves. "Aarohi, come in! What's up?"

I sat down across from her "Tanya, do you have ten minutes? I need to talk to you about something important."

She raised an eyebrow, curiosity sparking in her eyes. "Of course. What's on your mind?"

I took a deep breath and handed her the letter. "I'm resigning," I said softly. "I'll serve my full notice period, of course, but after that, I'll be leaving to pursue something I've been dreaming about for a long time."

Tanya looked at my resignation email, her eyes scanning the words. When she looked up, her expression was calm but serious. "What are you planning to do next?"

"I'm starting my own perfume business," I said, the words finally feeling real as they left my mouth. "It's something I've been working on for months now, and I think it's time I give it my full attention. I know it's a risk, but it's a risk I'm willing to take."

Tanya leaned back in her chair, a small smile playing on her lips. "Perfume, huh? That's interesting. And bold."

"It is," I admitted. "But it's something I'm passionate about. I've tested small batches, and the feedback has been incredible. I just... I want to see where this can go."

She nodded thoughtfully. "You've grown so much, Aarohi. I remember when you first joined, fresh out of college. And now, you're leaving as someone who knows exactly what she wants and isn't afraid to go after it. I'm proud of you."

Her words hit me harder than I expected, a lump forming in my throat. "Thank you, Tanya. For everything. You've been such a big part of my journey. I wouldn't be here without you."

Tanya reached across the table and squeezed my hand. "You're going to do great things, Aarohi. And when your perfume launches, I better be the first customer!"

We both laughed, the tension easing. As I left her cabin, a strange mix of emotions washed over me—gratitude, sadness, and an overwhelming sense of possibility.

# Chapter 31: Brotherhood

## Arjun

Fridays were usually a mess. But today was lighter. I had a single meeting on my calendar—Urban Bazaar's planning team had reached out weeks ago to request a Defense Services stall at their fair—an awareness slot for young students or curious visitors who wanted to know what it really meant to wear the uniform of the Armed forces.

As I walked into the conference room, I was mostly just ticking off checkboxes in my head. But then I saw the layout map on the projection screen—the entire Urban Bazaar spread out in sections. Homegrown brands. Food ventures. Women-led startups. I don't know what made me ask.

"Are stall bookings still open?"

The coordinator, a man in his late 30s, looked up and gave a quick shake of the head. "Sir, not even close. They were filled months ago. The screening process is tight. We had 1,400 applications and shortlisted 200. All finalised. Not unless someone drops out. And that's unlikely."

I nodded, pretending I didn't care.

But something about that last category—*women-led startups*—kept gnawing at me.

"Who's the regional director overseeing allocations?" I asked.

He scrolled through a file. "Mr. Rajiv Chauhan."

Rajiv Chauhan.

I pulled up the Urban Bazaar website and scrolled to the managing staff section. There he was—his photo under Regional Director. It's him. What are the odds?

Sainik School batchmate. Dorm mate. The guy I used to sneak into the canteen with to steal butter before anyone woke up for breakfast. The guy who faked my parents' signatures, took a punch without flinching.

We hadn't spoken in years, but that's the thing about boarding school bonds—they stay intact. They don't need constant check-ins. You just know they're there.

I stepped outside and dialled.

He picked up on the second ring.

"Abey Chowdhury!" Rajiv's voice boomed through the line, warm and unmistakably familiar. "Where the hell have you been, yaar?"

"On ship. Now stuck in a slight mess."

He laughed. "Same old. What do you need?"

"I need a stall at Urban Bazaar. Brand name: Nocturnal Essence. Woman-led perfume startup. Missed the registration deadline."

"You want a last-minute allocation in the busiest bazaar of the year?"

"I wouldn't ask if it wasn't important."

He didn't even blink.

"I'll give her one of the fallback sponsor slots?"

"Anything. I'll pay. I just need it done."

"Done," he said simply. "Send me the name, product category, and her founder profile if you have it. I'll slot her in."

"One more thing," I said, my voice a little lower. "Can you have the confirmation email sent directly to her? From the Urban Bazaar official ID. Make it sound like she's been selected on merit. Emphasize women-led ventures, community support, whatever you usually say. Just... don't make it look like a favour."

"I just don't want her to know it came from me."

There was a brief silence.

Then Rajiv said, "I'll take care of it."

"Send me the payment details."

"I'll WhatsApp it. Same number?"

"Yeah."

# Chapter 32: The Email

## Aarohi

I was halfway through cleaning out my office desk—old client notebooks, sticky notes with half-written to-dos, and the last of my Evora Events lanyards—when my phone buzzed.

*Subject: Selection Confirmation – Urban Bazaar Delhi 2021*

I blinked.

Wait... what?

I opened the email.

*Dear Ms. Aarohi Sinha,*

*We are thrilled to inform you that your brand, Nocturnal Essence, has been selected as one of the featured women-led ventures for this year's Urban Bazaar Delhi.*

*Your product line will be showcased under our Emerging Women Entrepreneurs Pavilion, alongside select brands from across the country.*

*Please find attached your stall confirmation, along with stall layout details and onboarding documentation.*

*Congratulations!*

*– Urban Bazaar Organizing Committee*

I read it twice.

Then again.

I hadn't applied.

I *hadn't applied.*

My heart hammered in my chest, a strange blend of disbelief and joy rushing through me like a wave. I dropped everything on my desk and stood frozen for a second, the glow of the laptop screen reflecting off the tears suddenly welling in my eyes.

I hadn't even *thought* of applying. Between the perfume orders, testing new blends, and the full-time chaos of Evora, it had felt impossible to squeeze in one more thing.

But now?

Now that I had resigned, cleared my last week, handed over all my projects, and stepped away for good...

This?

This was a sign.

The timing couldn't have been more perfect if I had prayed for it. I looked up at the ceiling, palms clasped in a folded thank-you.

"Thank you, thank you, thank you Universe," I whispered.

I pulled out my phone and opened the group chat.

**Me:** *Guys... I GOT SELECTED FOR URBAN BAZAAR!*

**Me (again):** *LIKE. I DIDN'T EVEN APPLY?? HOW IS THIS HAPPENING!*

Meher replied almost instantly.

**Meher:** *ARE YOU KIDDING ME.*

**Meher:** *THIS IS HUUUUUGE.*

Siya followed, all caps.

**Siya:** *START THE CHECKLISTS RIGHT NOW, WHATEVER YOU WOULD NEED.*

**Siya:** *THIS IS YOUR MOMENT.*

Maybe it is, I thought.

I clicked on the email again, reading it like it might vanish if I blinked.

I didn't know how or who or why this had happened.

But it had.

And all I knew was—I was going to make the most of it.

..................................................................................

This was it. I was at one of Delhi's most buzzing lifestyle events—*Urban Bazaar*. My friends, Siya and Meher had rallied around me, insisting they'd help me run the stall I had booked.

The air buzzed with the aroma of food trucks, chai stalls, and artisanal goods. My table stood neatly arranged with trial packs of the perfumes, tiny tester strips, and the full-sized bottles glimmering under the warm fairy lights. Siya was in charge of logistics, she took care of engaging conversations with visitors, and Meher was on fire with her social media pitch.

*"Don't forget to follow us on Instagram! Tag us when you post your stories,"* Meher chirped at every visitor.

Girls came and tried the perfumes, curious and intrigued. Each time someone sprayed a bottle and smiled, I felt my heart swell. It was working. My dream was coming to life. The feedback was overwhelmingly positive.

As the day slowly began to wind down, Meher walked up to me.

"Aarohi," she said gently, handing me a cream-colored envelope. I looked at her, confused.

She hesitated for a second, then added, "Arjun gave this to me... for you."

My breath caught.

"What?" I blinked, staring at the envelope.

"He stopped by the stall," Meher said, her voice low. "But he didn't want to distract you. Said he didn't want to mess with your energy today. Just asked me to make sure this reached you."

I looked down at the envelope in my hands.

# Chapter 33: Grateful

## Aarohi

The last two weeks felt like a blur, a slow and heavy one, the kind that drags your heart down with it. My days were filled with the perfume event preparations, endless trials, and sleepless nights. It kept me occupied. It kept me away from my thoughts of him.

But tonight, sitting on my bed, surrounded by the silence of my room and the faint hum of the city outside, I felt the weight of everything again. The day had been a success—the event went better than I imagined. Meher, Siya cheered me on like I'd already conquered the world.

I opened my journal. Writing always brought clarity to the chaos within me. I jotted down my gratitude for the day:

*"Dear Universe,*

*Thank you for this day. Thank you for the women who supported me, for the laughter we shared, and for the courage you've given me to chase my dreams. Thank you for the people who stopped by, who smiled, who said my perfumes made them happy. Thank you for reminding me that even when I feel lost, there's a path waiting for me. Thank you for always being there for me. I'm truly blessed, grateful and thankful to you. "*

I smiled faintly as I closed the journal. My eyes landed on the envelope Arjun had given me earlier that day. My heart tightened. I had shoved it into my bag without a second glance, refusing to open it at the moment. But now, I reached for it, my fingers hesitant as they traced the edges.

### *"Aarohi,*

*I don't know how to begin this. I've tried. I've rewritten this letter more times in my head than I can count, and every version still feels too small. Too little. Nothing I say will undo what I did, and I know that. But not saying it... not acknowledging the hurt I caused you, would be worse.*

*The past two weeks have been the hardest of my life. My legs won't recover the way I hoped. The rods are permanent–at least until the doctors say otherwise. And what I feel about it doesn't matter anymore. I've started the process of transferring to a new cadre. Soon, I'll be posted on a ship. Back on the water. Back to sailing. But before I leave, I have to find a way to reach you.*

*Because what I did... walking away that night without a word... that's not something I can carry with me. Not when you've given me nothing but love, patience, and a kind of presence I never believed I deserved.*

*When I met you, Aarohi, I was still buried under the weight of my past. I didn't know how to let go of it. I was chasing closure with someone who had already walked away, and I was too broken to recognize what I had in front of me. You didn't just care. You saw me. You sat with me in silence when I couldn't speak. You stood next to me without asking for anything in return. You made me feel like I could be more than what was left of me. I didn't know how to hold that. I didn't know how to be held like that.*

*I ran because I thought I still owed something to Ishita. I thought I was being honorable, facing the past. But the truth is, I wasn't running toward her. I was running from you. From the part of me that had already started to fall in love with you and didn't know how to handle it. And when I saw her again, I knew. My heart wasn't hers anymore. It hasn't been for a long time. It's yours, Aarohi. It's always been yours. I just didn't know how to say it until now.*

*I remember you once told me that gratitude makes everything bigger. That saying thank you can change how the world feels. I never told you this, but those words stayed with me. When the nights felt too heavy, when I was drowning in regret, it was your voice that I heard. "Thank you is enough." You taught me that. You taught me so much, and I never told you how deeply I carry your words.*

*I don't know if you'll ever forgive me. I don't know if you'll ever let me close again. But if you do... if there's even the smallest space left for me in your world, I'll do everything I can to earn it. I'll show you that I can be the man who doesn't run. The man who stays. The man who listens, who learns, who holds what matters instead of pushing it away.*

*I love you, Aarohi. With all that I am, even the broken pieces I'm still trying to put back together. And if you let me, I'll spend whatever time I have left becoming someone worthy of standing beside you.*

*Always,*

**Arjun"**

# Chapter 34: Say It. Mean It. Bleed It.

## Aarohi

The rain had been relentless.

It had been pouring for hours. I was still sitting on my bed with lights off, the room dimly lit by the flicker of the streetlamp outside my window. My legs ached from standing all day at the exhibition. My heart ached for reasons I didn't even want to name anymore.

I was still wearing my event tee, perfume stains on the sleeve, the scent of my own creation lingering on my wrist. Everyone had left. The stall was packed. The Urban Bazaar was over.

But I was still stuck in the moment Arjun walked out.

I stood by the balcony door now, staring at the glass blurred with rain. The city felt far away, like I'd been locked out of my own life. My body was still, but inside, everything was loud—clashing memories, unsent messages, the dull ache of heartbreak that couldn't even scream properly.

My breath caught. Through the rain, a shape came into focus.

Standing under the streetlight across the road.

**Arjun.**

I grabbed an umbrella and rushed outside, tiptoeing just enough to stretch it over his head.

"Are you stupid?" I snapped, half breathless. "You'll get sick; come inside."

He didn't say anything. Just followed me quietly. Not that the umbrella made much of a difference. He was already drenched. And in trying to cover him, I'd soaked myself too.

Water dripped from his sleeves, pooling around his shoes. His clothes clung to him like second skin, and the slight tremble in his fingers.

He pushed open the door to my house. We just stood there—me, holding the door; him, dripping onto the tiles.

Then, quietly, he said, "I've been standing there for 40 minutes. I didn't know if I should come up."

My throat tightened. I didn't answer.

"I tried calling," he added. "You didn't pick up."

I looked at him, too afraid to meet his eyes, and said quietly, "I was tired. Didn't look at my phone. Maybe it was on silent... I don't know."

He looked at me, and in that moment, I saw the pride in him break. And I hated myself for it.

Somehow, it felt like I made this happen. Like *I* had brought him to this.

He took a step forward, and then another, until he was just inches away.

And then he dropped to his knees and the moment he did, I forgot how to breathe.

"I don't deserve to be here," he said, looking up at me with eyes more vulnerable than I had ever seen. "But I needed to come anyway."

His voice cracked on the last word.

"I'm sorry," he whispered. "I'm so sorry, Aarohi."

He reached for my hand, hesitated... then gently took it. Cold skin against warm. Shaking fingers.

Then he kissed my knuckles—softly, reverently—like he was afraid even that would break me more.

"I broke everything," he said. "I walked away when I should've stayed. I said nothing when you gave me everything."

I stood there, frozen.

"I thought I owed something to my past. That if I didn't face it, I'd never be free. But the truth is... I wasn't running to Ishita. I was running from you. Because being with you felt too good, too real. And I didn't know how to hold something that wasn't born out of pain."

He looked down, rain still dripping from his hair to the floor.

"I saw her again. And in that moment, I knew. I didn't love her. I hadn't for a long time. I was just used to carrying her ghost around. But it was never her who made me feel alive again. It was you. It's always been you."

He stood slowly, stiff from the cold, still drenched.

He looked at me like he was trying to memorize my face.

He said, breaking again. "I walked out. I chose silence. I chose fear. But I never stopped loving you."

The words hung in the air like smoke.

"I'm leaving for sailing. It's 54 days at sea. I catch my flight in three hours and report to my next posting."

A pause.

"But I couldn't leave without seeing you. Without saying it. Without owning up to how badly I failed you."

I still didn't speak. But my eyes were burning now.

He steadied himself with the strength of my arm, then slowly stood. His hand reached for my face and when he looked at me, his eyes were red.

"I love you, Aarohi. Even if I never deserve to say it again. Even if you never say it back. Even if this is the last time we stand in the same room."

He hesitated.

"I'll wait for you... until you can forgive me."

I don't know where the strength came from, to stand tall in front of him, but somehow, I did.

My voice, steady but low, finally broke the silence.

"Why?"

He held my gaze.

"Because when something feels like home, you don't walk away—you wait until the door opens again."

The rain behind him poured like a curtain.

He stepped into it.

But just before the door shut, he looked at me—straight into my eyes.

"Next time I say I love you to you...

you'll feel it in every cell of your body."

And then the door clicked shut.

And it burned through every part of me.

# Chapter 35: If Love Had an Off Switch

## Aarohi

I didn't move for a long time after the door shut.

The silence in the apartment felt louder than the rain outside. It clung to the walls, to the folds of my t-shirt, to the floor where a trail of rainwater still glistened from where he had stood.

Only the streetlight flickered against the wet pavement, and the rain kept falling like it didn't know anything had changed.

I stood there, hugging myself, trying to breathe. But something inside me was hollow—like a space that used to be filled with rage had now been replaced by ache.

I just felt... *still*.

I walked back in, shutting the door softly behind me. The apartment was quiet. The kind of quiet that doesn't soothe—it suffocates.

I went to the kitchen. Boiled water for tea I didn't really want. Stared at the kettle as it screamed.

Everything in me wanted to forgive him.

But there was a part of me that was still stuck under that canopy—surrounded by fairy lights and melted candle wax—still waiting for him to come back.

Still waiting for the version of him who wouldn't leave.

*I wish love worked like a switch.*

*Off. Gone.*

*No echoes in the walls, no scent on my sweatshirt.*

*No ghosts when I say your name.*

*I wish my skin didn't remember you.*

*Wish my heart would stop rewinding,*

*Searching for the moment you stopped choosing me.*

*The shift was so quiet,*

*I didn't know I was losing you*

*Until there was nothing left to hold.*

*I wish I could hate you.*

*It'd be easier than this silence that still carries your voice.*

*This ache that won't let go,*

*No matter how many times I tell it to.*

*I wish I could go back to who I was before you.*

*Before love became a wound I kept touching.*

*But if forgetting were easy,*

*I wouldn't still be here—*

*Curled up in the wreckage,*

*Wishing I had never known you at all.*

# Chapter 36: Maggie

## Aarohi

It was barely light out, that soft, smoky kind of morning where the world still feels half-asleep. My hair was a mess, tied in a lazy knot that had mostly collapsed, and I was still in my pajamas—an old tee with "Not Today" printed across it and navy polka-dotted shorts. I had no intention of facing the world just yet.

Today was work.

I had orders lined up—bottles to wrap, thank-you notes to handwrite, fragrance kits to seal. The apartment smelled like lavender, jasmine, and vetiver, all mixing into a strange sort of calm.

I emailed Devika Rao, the venture capitalist—the woman I'd once pitched to with trembling hands and a folder full of dreams. I told her I resigned from Evora Events. That I was choosing *this*. That I was all in for my dream, Nocturnal Essence.

It felt like jumping off a ledge. But it also felt... *right*.

Just as I was printing shipping labels, the doorbell rang.

I opened the door, half-expecting Siya or a parcel guy from the courier service. Instead, a man stood there holding a wooden casket, with a soft blanket draped over it.

"Is this Aarohi's residence?" he asked.

"Uh... yes."

"Are you Aarohi?"

"Yeah."

He smiled and gently placed the casket in my hands. "This is for you."

I looked down—and froze.

Inside the basket, nestled on the softest pink blanket, was a golden retriever puppy.

Small. Fluffy. Brown-eyed.

She blinked up at me like she already knew me.

There was a bouquet tucked beside her. A wild mix of roses—red, white, yellow, and pink. And a folded letter.

She moved. Tipped forward a little. And those eyes—God, those tiny, liquid eyes—looked into mine and something cracked open inside my chest.

"Oh my God," I whispered. "Oh my God. You're so small."

I dropped to my knees right there by the doorway, my hair falling in my face, my hands fumbling to scoop her out gently.

"Are you hungry?" I murmured. "Do you want something to eat? Oh my god, you're *so cute.*"

She let out the tiniest yawn.

I scrambled inside, holding her close, nearly slipping on the floor as I rushed to the kitchen.

I placed the bowl of curd down and she dipped her nose in immediately, tail wagging.

While she ate, I finally noticed the letter again. My hands were trembling as I opened it.

### *Aarohi,*

*I've been trying to get her to you for a week now. Delays, confusion—but I hope she found you when you needed her.*

*If you haven't forgiven me yet, maybe she arrived at just the right time anyway. I hope she reminds you of the good parts. I hope she gives you the kind of love you once gave me—gentle, patient, real.*

*There's something I never told you.*

*Back when I was admitted in the military hospital, my bed was by the window. Every morning—every single morning at 5:45 AM—I'd see you running past on the road outside. You always had a few chapatis tucked into your running pouch. And like clockwork, you'd stop at the same corner and feed the stray dogs waiting for you. You'd talk to them, sometimes even dance a little with your earbuds in. I don't know what song it was but watching you from that window became my daily ritual. It gave me something to wait for.*

*One day, you found her. A golden retriever—older, hurt, barely moving. She'd clearly been abused. Probably bred too many times, then dumped like she didn't matter. You were crying, Aarohi. I watched you fall apart right there in the middle of the street, shouting at the watchman, asking him how he let this happen. I saw you storm off and come back minutes later with your car. I saw you scoop her up with shaking hands and drive her somewhere—probably the vet.*

*I know you loved her. And I know you lost her.*

*So maybe this little one isn't a replacement. No life can be.*

*But I thought... Maybe she deserves a better story, and I know you'll give her a home filled with more love than any breeder ever would.*

*Give her your music. Your dancing mornings. Your leftover chapatis.*

*She'll give you everything else.*

*Let me know what you name her. I'd love to know.*

### *- Arjun*

The tears came before I could stop them.

I looked at her again. She had finished the curd and was now licking the floor beside the bowl like she'd discovered heaven.

I crouched down beside her, pulled her into my lap, and whispered:

"Your name's Maggie."

I'd always known.

Since I was a teenager.

If I ever had a dog, her name would be Maggie.

Because Maggie Noodles stayed with you on late nights when no one else did. Maggie was comfort food. Maggie kept my company at midnight. Maggie never left.

I reached for my phone, still on the kitchen counter.

Typed:

Her name is Maggie.

Hit send.

One tick.

Just one tick.

He was already gone. Out for sailing, and out of network.

I looked down at Maggie, who had now curled up like a fluffy comma against my leg.

And I said softly, "It's okay. We'll figure it out."

# Chapter 37: Life Goes On

## Aarohi

It's been a month since Arjun left for sailing.

And life? It hasn't stopped for even a second.

My days now begin early—sometimes with the rustling sound of Maggie pouncing onto the bed, other times with a calendar notification pinging me awake before the sun has even decided to show up. The apartment smells like bergamot and lavender most mornings, a reminder that this little dream of mine—*Nocturnal Essence*—is finally becoming something real.

A week ago, I had a second meeting with Devika—the investor I'd pitched to all those weeks back. This time, I didn't come in nervous. I came in ready. She smiled when I finished and simply said, "You've grown into your story, Aarohi."

I didn't cry in front of her. But when I got home, and Maggie licked my face while I was still on the floor with my heels on— I did. Because we did it. I signed my first seed investment. It's not just a brand anymore. It's a business.

The feedback has been incredible. Some customers wrote paragraphs about how a scent reminded them of their childhood courtyard, or their wedding. That's the thing about perfume—it never just sits on the skin. It *lives* in memory.

I've hired two people now. Riya's a genius with reels, captions, and turning even my clumsiest workspace photos into trending content. And Savidha—my calm in the chaos—has taken over inventory like she was born to organize.

That's given me the time to focus on what I love most—blending. Quietly. Carefully. Alone, often at night, when the world is quieter, and the oils feel like they're whispering.

The Pinkathon marathon is a month away. My long-distance runs have become non-negotiable. 10K practice on Tuesdays. Hill work on Fridays. On Sundays, I go to Nehru Park before sunrise. Maggie sometimes tags along for the cooldown lap.

And yet, there are days...

When I pass that Bangla Sahib turn, or cross the Navy accommodation gate—he floods back.

Arjun.

There are days when the ache creeps in unexpectedly—like a song you didn't even realise was still on your playlist. On those days, I open my private WhatsApp chat. I hit a record. I speak.

Sometimes it's just, "I passed by Bangla Sahib today... crossed our usual spot."

Sometimes it's a full monologue about my day I want to share with him.

But I still record. Everything I want to say to him—*I keep it there.*

He calls when he gets network. Sometimes I answer. Sometimes I miss it, and by the time I call back—he's out of network again. He once told me that there are only a few spots on deck that catch signals, and when he stands there, he waits. Just in case I call back.

Sometimes, when I miss Arjun, I think about all the Naval wives who live like this—not just for weeks, but for years. I wonder how strong they must be to spend so many nights alone, raising children who only see their fathers in bursts of time—maybe a video call, a few days of leave, and then back to waiting. I wonder how it must feel to tuck your child into bed knowing their dad is somewhere out there, in the middle of the ocean, serving the country. It's easy to love when they're beside you. The real test is when they're oceans away—and you still set two plates at dinner. It takes a different kind of strength to hold that space—to love someone who's always leaving, and still trust they'll come back.

It humbles me. Because for them, love in their world isn't in the holding— it's in the waiting.

Because sometimes, love doesn't sit beside you on the couch. Sometimes, love is standing on the jetty, watching a ship disappear—and still smiling when it returns.

This morning, while working on packaging a custom order, I got a text from Abhay.

*"Hey Aarohi, hope you're good. Need to talk about the Ironman plan. Can we catch up?"*

I stared at the message longer than I should've.

Ironman. It's in 3.5 months. I am participating in a relay with Arjun and Abhay.

He texted again:

*"Let's meet at Zephyr Café this evening if you're free. I've got the logistics sorted—travel, hotel, gear. I'm coordinating with Arjun too,*

*he said he's good with whatever works for you. Just want to know your preferences so we can lock it all in."*

So now, I'm meeting Abhay in the evening.

There's so much to say, but I don't even know what I feel yet.

All I know is that life has been moving forward.

And I've been moving with it.

But some days... I still look back where everything was perfect.

# Chapter 38: The Dialect of Silence

## Aarohi

Zephyr Café always smelled of cinnamon mingled with Delhi's late-spring air—dry, a little dusty, and tinged with the scent of flowering gulmohars —a comforting irony for a conversation I wasn't quite ready for. I'd arrived early, secretly hoping Abhay might cancel at the last moment. But deep down, I knew he wouldn't.

He walked in precisely two minutes past five, his white linen shirt crisply tailored, sleeves casually rolled to reveal tan lines that spoke of long days under relentless sun. His smile was gentle, quietly reassuring.

"Hey," he greeted softly, sliding into the seat across from me. "I hope I didn't keep you waiting."

"Not at all," I lied lightly, easing into the familiar charade.

We ordered cold brews and a plate of fries to share, the comfort of fries could make the world's chaos feel momentarily bearable.

Initially, we stayed safe, dancing around the practicalities.

"I'm being posted to Agra in two months," Abhay announced casually. "We'll all meet directly in Goa. Ironman's shaping up nicely—Arjun's on the swim, I'm cycling, and you..." He paused meaningfully. "You better be ready to run like hell."

I allowed myself a smile. "I'm training, don't worry."

"Good," he grinned. "I've already booked the slots. You're in too deep to back out now."

"Wouldn't dream of it," I said quietly, almost genuinely.

Then came the inevitable pivot.

"You still haven't forgiven him, have you?" he asked, his voice gentle but unwavering.

I took refuge in my coffee, the silence stretching comfortably between us. Abhay didn't rush me; his profession made him understand silence better than most.

"He asks about you," he continued softly, his eyes steady on mine. "He'd deny it, of course, but you're there in every conversation, one way or another."

Something inside me tightened painfully.

"He doesn't talk easily," Abhay admitted. "He buries everything deep. But the first time I saw him cry in years was after the night he left you at that canopy."

I swallowed, the ache sharp in my throat. I blinked away the sting behind my eyes, struggling to hold the pieces of myself together.

"Can I ask you something personal?" Abhay's tone was careful, searching.

I nodded faintly, unsure but willing to trust him.

"What exactly did you feel when he left you there?"

The question startled me; I hadn't even dared to ask it myself. Yet the answer rushed out before I could reconsider. "I felt...unworthy. Not beautiful enough. When he left, my mind instantly compared me to her—to how he'd described her before. And suddenly, I wasn't good enough."

The confession hung raw between us, the truth cutting deeper spoken aloud. I hadn't expected to bare this part of myself, especially not to Abhay. But it was done.

Abhay leaned in, his voice low and deliberate. "You know what's tragic, Aarohi? That we've become a generation obsessed with our own reflections. We stare at mirrors, filters, screens—constantly measuring, comparing, correcting. Imagine if mirrors had never existed. Imagine if we weren't supposed to see ourselves this much. Maybe then, beauty wouldn't feel like a battlefield."

He let the silence settle for a moment before saying my name, softer this time—like he was walking into fragile territory.

"Aarohi... no one else has the power to make you feel unworthy. Not him. Not her. That feeling—it doesn't start with them. It starts with us. We hand people the knife and then blame them for the cut. The truth is, it's our own insecurities we quietly project onto the people we love— expecting them to heal what they never broke."

I looked away, recognizing the truth in his words— and somehow, hearing it from someone else made it harder to breathe.

"The fundamental difference between men and women," he continued quietly, "is our language of love. Women find solace in words; they want to express, dissect, and share. Men, especially those of us in defence, retreat when emotions overwhelm us. We step away to regain clarity."

He paused, ensuring I was still with him. I met his eyes, hesitant but open.

"Tell me honestly," he pressed gently. "What's the one fear holding you back from forgiving him?"

My voice trembled as I answered, "What if she returns? What if he leaves me again—what if he cheats on me?"

He considered this quietly before speaking. "Are you willing to sacrifice what could be, based on a 'what if'? If you truly believe in manifestation, Aarohi, why focus on outcomes you don't desire? Why let fear dictate your future?"

I took a deep breath, feeling the tightness slowly easing from my chest. "Abhay, I genuinely want to forgive him. Every part of me does. But I don't know how. How do I make myself forgive him when my mind is constantly fighting inner battles? My heart wants to let go, but my mind... it keeps replaying everything like it's stuck in a loop I can't shut off."

Abhay's voice softened further "Forgiveness isn't a switch, Aarohi. It won't happen overnight. It's a journey—days, weeks, maybe longer. Give yourself the grace to feel your hurt, understand your fears. But don't let pride slam shut a door your heart is still standing before."

I looked at Abhay and nodded.

The silence between us felt softer now, warmer somehow.

And sitting across from him—I felt a little less alone.

# Chapter 39: In Every Version of You

## Aarohi

The wind had picked up slightly as I stepped out of Zephyr Café. I didn't speak to Abhay after that. We said our goodbyes in silence.

I sat in my car, keys unmoved in the ignition, and stared ahead at the fading light. The street was half-empty, the sky wearing those in-between shades.

I picked up my phone and tapped on his name.

Arjun.

Out of network. Again. Of course.

I sighed and opened my private WhatsApp chat.

The place I said all the things I never had the courage to send.

I tapped the mic button. It blinked red. I began.

"*Hi...*" I whispered, my voice barely above a breath.

"*You're not going to hear this today. Probably not tomorrow either. But someday, maybe.*"

I looked out at the road, my eyes already stinging.

"*I don't know when I stopped being angry. Maybe somewhere between training runs and perfume batches, I just... got tired. Of being angry. Of missing you with a clenched heart.*"

I laughed lightly. It broke halfway through.

*"You remember when I told you... love is in the staying?"*

I paused.

*"Well... I stayed. Even when I said I wouldn't. Even when I pretended, I had walked away. I stayed with your words. With the way you looked at me. With the way you said sorry like you meant it more than anything else you've ever said."*

A long silence stretched on the recording.

Then—

*"I don't know how to say this, so I'll just... say it."*

*"I love you, Arjun."*

*"I love you in the most terrifying, quiet, inconvenient ways. I love you in every version you've ever been—even the ones that hurt me. And I don't know what that says about me, but it's true."*

I swallowed hard.

*"So, this isn't a confession. Or a plea. It's just... a moment. One I needed to say out loud."*

I looked down at my lap, voice barely a whisper now.

*"So... Thank you. For making me feel. For breaking me open. For showing me that love can survive even when it's not returned right away."*

The voice note ticked past two minutes.

*"I'll see you soon. Whenever that is."*

I ended the recording.

And hit send—to myself. As always.

# Chapter 40: My First Marathon!

## Aarohi

My legs were screaming.

The moment I hit the 35 km mark; it was like my body stopped obeying me. My breath came in short, uneven gasps. My calves were seizing up, and that familiar sharp cramp settled into my side, spreading fast. I had trained but nothing prepares you for this—when your body refuses to move even one step further. They say, Training is the marathon; the race is the celebration. Nothing about this felt celebratory.

I slowed to a walk. My hands on my hips, sweat dripping off my jaw. My mouth was dry, but water felt like it would make me puke. I wiped my face with the back of my wrist, breath catching in my throat. There were runners ahead, fading behind, volunteers shouting encouragement, someone waving a banana at me from the side.

But all I could hear was my heartbeat hammering inside my head.

I bent slightly, trying to catch my breath.

Maybe I should stop. Just five minutes. Sit down. Rest. Anything. My vision blurred and my chest felt tight. Somewhere between the blur of cramps and the pounding in my ears, I caught the faintest trace of something familiar. That scent—his. It came with the wind, subtle but enough to make me lift my head. I could already feel him close to me.

"Aarohi."

My head jerked up.

Arjun.

He wasn't wearing a race bib. Just track pants, a faded Navy tee, and a water bottle in his hand. His hair was damp from sweat or the humidity, and his chest was rising and falling like he'd been running.

He must've jumped in from the crowd.

"I saw you slowing down," he said, voice quiet but sure. "Thought I'd run the rest with you. Just match my pace. Don't think about anything else—just the next step. One, two. One, two."

I couldn't speak.

I just nodded. It was either that or cry.

I matched his pace.

One step. Another. Match him.

The noise faded, like the world has been put on mute—just the sound of our feet on pavement and the blood pounding in my ears.

"Here," he said, offering his bottle.

I took a small sip and handed it back, the water burning down my dry throat.

"You, okay?" he asked.

"No," I whispered. "But I want to finish."

"You will."

Another kilometer passed. And another. My legs were jelly now, trembling with every step, my arms swinging more from desperation than momentum. I wanted to stop. I wanted to scream. I wanted to collapse.

"Just focus on the next step," he said softly. "Don't think about the finish line. Just this next one."

And I did.

My body felt like a war zone. My thighs burned. My stomach twisted. My brain screamed for mercy. But his voice was the one that pulled me forward—again and again.

"You've got this."

"Keep going"

I lost track of time. The noise came back in waves. Cheering. Banners. The announcer's voice echoing in the distance.

And then I saw it.

The finish line.

Just ahead.

My lips parted, a choked breath escaping. I pushed harder, every muscle on the verge of giving out.

Arjun slowed down, stepping out of the path. He clapped hard, yelling, "You got this! Go!" It was the last 100 meters left maybe.

And then I crossed it.

Just like that, it was done, I completed my first marathon, my very first marathon! It felt so good!

My legs gave out and I staggered, falling forward into him. He caught me instantly, arms wrapping around me, holding me up and I couldn't hold it in anymore. I cried. Finally—I had my marathon medal.

"I did it," I gasped, tears spilling. "I did it."

"You did it. You're a marathoner."

I laughed and cried at the same time; face buried against his chest.

He didn't let go.

# Chapter 41: Post Marathon!

## Aarohi

My heart hadn't stopped racing since the finish line.

Not from the run—God, no. That part was long done. I'd survived 42.2 km, cramps, the sun on my back.

No. This was something else.

This was Arjun. We stayed tangled in that hug longer than necessary—his breath still heavy against my temple, my legs barely able to hold me up. When he finally pulled back, his palms lingered at my waist, grounding me. My chest rose and fell in shallow bursts, still catching up.

"You need to stretch, otherwise you will be sore" he said, voice low, soft.

"I can't move," I muttered, half-laughing, half-dizzy.

We walked a few steps to a quieter corner of the park, away from the marathon crowd. The grass was patchy, a little damp. I sat down, slowly, legs trembling beneath me. Arjun crouched beside me. He didn't speak, just reached for my left leg, lifting it gently onto his thigh.

I flinched. Just the shock of skin on skin. My body was hypersensitive, raw from the run, and his hands felt impossibly warm.

He pressed my foot forward, keeping the stretch firm but careful. One hand cradled my ankle, the other slid up to hold my thigh steady. The space between us narrowed. I could feel the fabric of his t-shirt graze my arm, the muscle under his fingers flex as he held me in place.

"Too much?" he asked.

I shook my head. "No. Just... intense."

Arjun knelt down in front of me. I stiffened slightly, unsure of what he was doing, until he reached for my foot and started untying my shoelace. I sat there, frozen. He removed the shoe, then pulled off the sock.

My feet must smell terrible. This is so embarrassing.

I wanted to pull away, say something, stop him—but I didn't. Because the moment his thumb pressed into the arch of my foot, all that awkwardness blurred. His hands were warm, and he knew exactly where to apply pressure. My body started to relax without my permission.

He moved up to my calf, gently pressing along the tight muscle, and I could feel every bit of the tension from the run slowly giving in. I let my elbows fall behind me for support, trying not to make eye contact.

Then he reached for the other foot. Same thing—shoe, sock, and then those same careful hands. It was almost too much, the way it made me feel. I didn't know how to ask him to stop. I didn't want to.

"You must be hungry," he said, voice warm, familiar.

I nodded too fast. "Starving."

He smirked gently. "McDonald's?"

"Yes!!!!!!!!!!!!!!!!!!!!!!"

"I knew it," he grinned, shaking his head. "Come on."

The car was quiet. Too quiet.

We were passing the McDonald's when I spoke. "Can we just take it home? Eat there?"

He looked at me for a second, then nodded. "Yes, I can meet Maggie too!"

I smiled. "Yeah. She'll be excited to see you."

His voice softened. "Yeah. I really want to meet her."

Maggie was waiting like she *knew*. The door barely opened, and she launched into wags and soft barks and the kind of excitement that was reserved for people you know deep in your bones.

She went straight to Arjun. Not me.

"Oh, okay," I said, laughing, "she doesn't even care that I'm here."

He knelt, gathering her in his arms, pressing kisses to her furry little forehead.

"I missed you too," he whispered to her, laughing as she tried to climb him.

I walked to the kitchen, unwrapping the burgers, placing fries in bowls. As I reached for the plates, I felt it—his presence behind me, he was standing close enough that I could feel the heat of his breath

He didn't touch me. But I felt him—in the warmth of his breath, the nearness of his body. It was enough to make my breath hitch.

"Aarohi," he said, his voice low. Almost reverent.

I turned. Slowly.

He was so close.

"I'm sorry," he whispered. "I know I've said it before. But I need you to know—I mean it. I mean it with everything I have left."

"I've already forgiven you, Arjun," I said, my voice barely above a whisper.

His eyes lit up like I'd handed him the stars. There was something boyish in that smile—hopeful, undone.

"You didn't tell me," he said, half laughing, half breathless.

"Wait," I said, turning to the phone on the table. I opened my private WhatsApp chat, handed it to him. "Play the last one."

He looked down. Saw the voice notes. Hesitated.

And then he played it.

My voice filled the room. Soft. Raw. Honest.

*"I love you in the most terrifying, quiet, inconvenient ways. I love you in every version you've ever been—even the ones that hurt me. And I don't know what that says about me, but it's true."*

He stared at the screen for a second, frozen.

Then he put it down gently and stepped forward. His arms wrapped around me, and he whispered close to my ear,

"Sweetheart, you know... when a message is meant for someone, you're supposed to send it to them. Messages don't exactly deliver themselves."

I let out a small laugh.

And then he kissed me.

Like every damn wall between us had finally crumbled.

Like the months apart had been leading to this exact second.

His mouth on mine. My hands gripped his shoulders. Our breath tangled.

He lifted me, sat me on the counter, stepped between my legs, and kissed me again—deeper this time. Hotter. Like he needed to map every inch of my mouth with his.

I felt breathless. Spun out. Whole.

He leaned his forehead against mine.

"Wait here."

He walked over to his bag, pulled out his phone, and tapped through something.

He brought it back. Handed it to me.

Emails. Dozens of them. All unsent. All addressed to me.

"I watched your stall video today. You were glowing."

"It's been 23 days, and I miss your voice like I'm starving."

"I drafted a reply to your silence six times today. None of them said enough."

"I love you. I still do. I don't know if you'll ever see this. But I do."

"It was our Commanding Officer's wife's birthday, so I showed him your business website and recommended it for her gifts. They absolutely loved your work. I felt so proud of you!"

Tears pooled in my eyes as I scrolled.

"You wrote all of these?" I whispered.

"I couldn't send them," he said. "But I needed to say it. Somewhere."

I looked up at him, biting back a smile.

"Sweetheart, you know... when a message is meant for someone, you're supposed to send it to them. Messages don't exactly deliver themselves."

And we both laughed—soft, messy, a little teary. And I kissed him again.

This time, slower. And then

Longer.

Deeper.

Like the silence between us had waited its whole life to be broken by this exact moment.

His lips moved with the kind of urgency that made my pulse stutter, his hands gripping my waist. I could feel everything—his breath, his heartbeat, the ache in him.

"I love you," he whispered between kisses.

Again.

And again.

And again.

Each time he said it, it sank deeper. Into my skin. Into my lungs. Into every cell that had been aching for this.

"I love you, Aarohi," he said, voice rough against my throat, his lips brushing the shell of my ear, "and this time, you're going to feel it everywhere."

And I did.

It wasn't just a kiss anymore—he was everywhere.

I pulled away for a second, needing to catch my breath, my fingers still curled around his collar.

"I must smell like sweat," I said, breathless, laughing softly as the reality of my post-run state hit me. "Let me just freshen up—take a quick shower."

His eyes dropped to my lips, then back up.

He stepped in closer.

"No."

Voice low. Certain.

"Let me."

He leaned in, barely a whisper between us.

"Let me come with you."

Before I could respond, his hands were already around me. I gasped—half laughing, half stunned—as he scooped me up. He kicked the door open gently. The moment we stepped inside, he set me down ... only to begin undressing me with eyes locked with mine.

My bare chest pressed to his soaked shirt. His hands moved rougher now, sliding down my back, cupping me hard as his mouth found my neck.

"Arjun..." I whispered.

He just kissed me again—harder this time.

And when his fingers slid between my thighs, there was no space left for anything else.

Just us.

# Epilogue: The Ironman

The sun was still rising over Goa when Arjun stepped into the water. His body moved through the waves along with other participants. Abhay and I stood at the sidelines, watching the screen, tracking his progress.

When he finally emerged—dripping, breathless—we clapped like crazy.

He handed the timing band to Abhay with a nod. There's a silent language between them that they both spoke fluently.

Abhay clipped in and took off on his bike. Arjun and I followed him along the route. At every checkpoint, every sharp turn, we cheered. We screamed his name till our throats hurt. Arjun kept his arm loosely around my waist.

When Abhay hit his final two kilometres, I sat on the edge of the track and double-knotted my laces.

Arjun bent slightly, pressed a kiss to my forehead.

"All the best," he said. "You've got this."

I took the band from Abhay, smiled, and started running.

The first 5 km were smooth. Then the sun started doing what it does in Goa—burn.

Still, at every bend, I'd see them—Arjun and Abhay.

Shouting my name.

Cheering like they were on fire.

By the 20th kilometre, my body was shaking, for the final kilometre they joined me. To finish it together.

Abhay on the left, Arjun on the right. We just matched our steps.

And in the final stretch, we held hands.

Three runners.

One finish line.

Together.

We crossed it in a blur of sweat, smiles, and something I'll never forget.

Abhay grinned, medal in hand.

"Next year—full individual Ironman?"

I looked at Arjun.

He smiled. "Maybe... let's do that."

# Bonus Chapter: After the Finish Line

The sun dipped low over Goa, leaving streaks of tangerine and blush in the sky. The crowd had started to thin out after the Ironman ceremony. Medals gleamed softly around necks, shoes powdered with beach sand, and someone strummed a guitar nearby.

Arjun nudged my shoulder. "You up for a walk?"

I nodded, slipping my fingers into his.

We strolled past the event arena, down toward the quieter side of the beach. Maggie had already been picked up by Abhay—he winked at me before taking her and whispering something in Arjun's ear. Arjun just smiled.

The tide had pulled back a little. I could see lanterns lining a stretch of the sand ahead. And then I saw it.

A canopy. Draped in white, lit with soft golden fairy lights. Tiny glass bottles with flowers hung from the frame. Candles flickered in the breeze. A pathway of shells and petals led straight to it.

I turned to Arjun, eyebrows raised. "What... is this?"

He didn't answer. Just held my hand tighter and led me toward it.

Inside the canopy, there was just a blanket, two cushions, and a low table with food, some fruits, and a bottle of wine.

He turned to me then.

Took both my hands.

And dropped to one knee.

For a second, everything went silent.

"Aarohi," he began, voice steady but low,

He looked down for a second, then back at me.

"You came into my life when I wasn't even looking for love—when I least expected to fall for someone... and you didn't try to fix me. You just saw me. *All* of me. And you stayed."

A pause.

"You've seen the darkest corners of my soul and still found reasons to love me. You've held space for the man I was and the one I'm trying to become. You fought for us—even when I didn't know how to."

He opened the box, revealing the ring.

"I don't know what life will look like in the coming years, or how many more storms we'll weather. But I do know this—there is no version of my life that makes sense without you in it."

His voice cracked a little now, but he didn't look away.

"I love you, Aarohi. *All* of you. Every part.

The loud. The quiet. The stubborn. The soft. The fire.

I love you when we're laughing. I love you when we're fighting. I love you when you walk away from me—and even more when you walk back."

He took a breath.

"I want every sunrise with you. Every ordinary day. Every chaos and every calm.

I want to build a life so full, so real, that even the hard days feel worth it—because you're in them."

He reached for my hand.

"So... will you marry me? Will you build this life with me—from wherever we are, with whatever we have, for as long as we're breathing?"

My hands flew to my face, a half-laugh, half-sob escaping my throat.

"Yes," I whispered. Then louder. "*Yes. Yes. Of course, I will.*" And before I could stop myself, a tiny, giddy dance-jump burst out of me.

He stood and slid the ring onto my finger, and before I could even pull him into a hug—

Fireworks lit up the sky.

I gasped as the first crack exploded in the air.

Pink. Gold. Violet. One after the other, blooming like flowers across the darkness. My face lit up with every burst.

I turned to him, stunned. "You planned *fireworks?*"

He grinned, slipping his arms around my waist. "You really think I'd propose to you without a little drama?"

I laughed through the tears, resting my forehead against his. "You're such a show-off."

He kissed my nose. "Only for you."

We stood there, wrapped in each other, under a sky bursting with color. The canopy lights flickered around us, the music played on, and somewhere in the distance, I swore I could hear the ocean smile.

I leaned into him, my fingers curled into his shirt.

And in that moment, with the sand under our feet, the stars above, and a future wide open in front of us—

I knew.

This wasn't just the end of a chapter.

This was the beginning of *forever*.

# Acknowledgements

To begin with, thank you to every reader who picked up this book—whether you read it in one sitting or over slow, quiet nights. Even if you loved it or hated it, I truly appreciate the time you gave to Aarohi and Arjun.

To Nitin, my love—none of this would exist without you. You didn't just inspire Arjun's character, you stood by me through every messy draft, every self-doubt spiral, every late-night ramble. You let me dream loud.

To Bella, our golden baby—you were there for it all. Lying under my desk while I typed. You were part of this story too, even if you didn't know it.

To my family and my girls—I don't even have the right words for you. Thank you for being the ones I could fall apart with. For holding me when I cried without reason, for celebrating every tiny win like it was everything, for showing up even when we didn't talk for days. You've seen me in my most unfiltered, unsure, and messy moments—and you never looked away.

To the version of me that was scared to begin—thank you for beginning anyway.

To our Indian Navy family—you've been our home away from home.

To the BlueRose Publishers team—this wouldn't have been possible without you. You made my little dream come true, and I'll always be grateful for that.

This isn't just a book.

It's a piece of my heart.

And I'm so grateful it made its way to you.

*With all my love,*

*Versha*

# About Author

Born and raised in Delhi, Versha Sangwan spends her days gracefully juggling corporate chaos, endless deadlines, and the quirky adventures of being married to a naval officer—where "anchors aweigh" often means dinner plans postponed. Between navigating office meetings and decoding navy life, she's come to firmly believe the universe takes joy in turning her carefully laid plans into amusing misadventures—which ultimately inspired her debut novel. If you've ever laughed when life took an unexpected U-turn or wondered if fate secretly enjoys messing with your calendar, you and Versha are going to get along just fine.

*Get in touch—she promises to reply faster than her Outlook inbox allows!*

📷: life_of_versha_sangwan

in: Versha Sangwan

www.ingramcontent.com/pod-product-compliance
Lightning Source LLC
LaVergne TN
LVHW041921070526
838199LV00051BA/2694